To Alan Ross

From an early age John Haylock was fascinated with abroad, in particular the East. He believes that one cannot properly know a place until one has set up house there. He has lived in Baghdad, Tokyo, Cyprus, Cairo, Tangier and Chiang Mai. *Doubtful Partners* is his sixth novel. With Desmond Stewart he wrote *New Babylon*, a portrait of Iraq in the fifties. He translated Philippe Jullian's *Flight into Egypt*, and, with Francis King, Jullian's biography of Robert de Montesquiou. His short stories have appeared in *Blackwoods Magazine, London Magazine, Winter's Tales* and *Short Story International.* In 1995 he was elected a Fellow of the Royal Society of Literature. *Eastern Exchange*, his memoirs, was published in 1998. He lives in Hove when he is not in the Far East.

BY THE SAME AUTHOR

Eastern Exchange: Memoirs
New Babylon: A Portrait of Iraq
(with Desmond Stewart)

NOVELS

See You Again
It's All Your Fault
One Hot Summer in Kyoto
A Touch of the Orient
Uneasy Relations

PUBLICATIONS IN JAPAN

Tokyo Sketchbook
Choice and other stories
Japanese Excursions
Japanese Memories
Romance Trip and other stories

TRANSLATIONS FROM THE FRENCH

Robert de Montesquiou by Philippe Jullian
(with Francis King)
Flight into Egypt by Philippe Jullian

DOUBTFUL PARTNERS

John Haylock

ARCADIA BOOKS
LONDON

Arcadia Books Ltd
15–16 Nassau Street
London W1N 7RE

First published in Great Britain 1998 © John Haylock

John Haylock has asserted his moral right to be identified as
the author of this work in accordance with the Copyright,
Designs and Patents Act, 1988

All Rights Reserved. No part of this publication may be
reproduced in any form or by any means without the prior
written permission of the publishers

A catalogue record for this book is available from the British Library

ISBN 1-900850-18-4

Arcadia Books distributors are as follows:

in the UK and elsewhere in Europe:
Turnaround Publishers Services
Unit 3, Olympia Trading Estate
Coburg Road
London N22 6TZ

in the USA and Canada:
Dufour Editions, Inc
PO Box 7
Chester Springs, PA
19425–0007

in Australia:
Tower Books
PO Box 213
Brookvale, NSW 2100

in New Zealand
Addenda
PO Box 78224
Grey Lynn
Auckland

Typeset in Garamond by M Rules
Printed and bound in Finland by WSOY

Part One

1

While Barbara Lane, her son Neville, and her daughter Jennifer were about to make their way to Chiang Mai to attend Henry Lane's funeral, Sylvia Field was arriving at her mother's apartment in Hove. Sylvia left Tokyo early on Christmas Eve, and although exhausted by the flight and the emotional strain she had been undergoing over the last fortnight, she did her best to appear bright on Christmas Day. Her mother, Mrs Gertrude Hawkins, was giving her annual Christmas luncheon to her 'fellow fogies', as she called her friends, all of whom were septuagenarians like herself.

Sylvia helped her mother prepare the traditional meal: roast turkey with the customary trimmings, Christmas pudding made in November, and tangerines, grapes, nuts and crystallised fruit – 'heavenly fruit' Sylvia had called it as a child. Two bottles of champagne were in the refrigerator. Mrs Hawkins served the same meal as her mother had given at Christmas and as she had given her late husband, a doctor, and Sylvia, her only child.

'You must be the sole person in Hove who ends a meal with fresh fruit,' remarked Sylvia to her mother. They were in the kitchen of the ninth-floor flat preparing potatoes and Brussels sprouts.

'It's the proper way to end a Christmas luncheon. We've always done so. It's a great joy to have you here, Sylvia dear, and as Violet Tysoe can't come – she's down with the flu – we'll be six as usual, the right number for the dining table. Seven, as we would have been if Violet could have come, is too much of a squeeze, so it's a good thing she can't, although of course I'm sorry she's not well; she sounded very hoarse on the phone.'

Sylvia wondered if her mother was really pleased at her sudden and unexpected arrival. Her departure from Japan had been precipitous. By chance there was a seat on a British Airways flight to London, and on a whim, had taken it. Now she was back in England after nine months away, she wondered whether she should stay in her native land or return to Tokyo. She ought to return and finish the academic year which ended in the middle of March, but since her contract had been curtailed, owing to the machinations of Professor Suzuki, she felt she was not under an obligation to do so. She had told Professor Maeda, who had found her a substitute job in a Japanese publishing firm, that she would let him know after the New Year holiday whether she would accept it or not. And there was Toshi, who had been her lover, but he was twenty-six and she was fifty; he had another mother figure anyway and his parents and the manager of the bank where he worked were pressing him to get married. It was better, Sylvia felt, to give up Japan and its complications, and yet . . .

2

During Mrs Hawkins's and Sylvia's morning preparations for the Christmas feast, the evening party which Matthew Bennet and Jun were giving in their exiguous Tokyo apartment for their friends was about to begin. It was eight p.m., and only Bill and his Japanese chum had arrived. Bill was American, tall and thirty-five; Minoru, his friend, was twenty, a student, slender, and he only came up to Bill's shoulder.

'Sylvia couldn't come,' Matthew informed Bill. 'She's flown to England.'

'I didn't know you'd invited her,' said Bill.

'Thought I ought to.'

Minoru joined Jun in the kitchen and animated Japanese chirping began.

'I rang to ask her,' continued Matthew, 'as Jun and I felt she'd be lonely on this supposedly festive day. Toshi has a bank party, a *bonen-kai*, you know, one of those year-end things salary men can't get out of. Well, I rang Sylvia and she told me she was going to England. Jun says she won't come back. I say she will. Professor Maeda has found another job for her.'

'It's a shame she was sacked.'

'Monstrous. All because of that shit Suzuki, whom she rebuffed.'

The bell rang.

'The others have come.' Matthew rose. 'Jun, the bell! The others have come!'

3

Arthit, the Thai paramour of Barbara's husband, was beside himself with grief after the accident in which Henry was killed on the morning of Christmas Day. It had not been his fault. Henry had suddenly told him to change direction as they were entering Chiang Mai and he had crashed his truck into a tree which was on the edge of the road, the old Chiang Mai-Lamphun road bordered for much of the way by majestic Dyptercarps. The gap between the trees and the ditch was used by vehicles, wrongly so, turning left to cross the Mangrai Bridge over the River Ping. Arthit should have gone round the tree; he didn't because it was easier not to. The left side of the truck had been badly smashed and Henry had been killed instantly. Miraculously Arthit had escaped injury. He had managed to extricate himself from the truck and summon help.

The police had arrived. Henry's body was taken to the mortuary and Arthit to the main police station, where he had been allowed to telephone his boss, Peter Cochrane, in Bangkok. Peter said he'd leave for Chiang Mai at once, and he would telephone Neville Lane, who he knew was at the family home: Grasslands, near Guildford. Peter Cochrane was the manager of the Thai branch of the British pharmaceutical company of which Henry Lane had been a senior member of the board in London.

4

Mrs Hawkins's guests had arrived and were assembled in the drawing-room as the old lady insisted on calling the sitting-room, an oblong modern room cluttered with antique furniture, porcelain vases and bowls which had mostly come from her and her husband's family homes, sold many years ago. The Georgian and Victorian cabinets and bureaux looked unhappy; they seemed to cry out in complaint at being in such inappropriate quarters. One bottle of champagne, which Gertrude had poured out, had already been consumed and the English reserve was melting. Sylvia, who had not yet greeted her mother's guests, was in the kitchen relieving her mother by making final preparations for the feast. She would not feel at ease with her mother's cronies, whom she had met before on her brief visits to Hove. What had she to say to Colonel Bernard Loxley and his wife or to Sir Geoffrey Hinton and his lady? All were now denizens of Hove and although they had led interesting lives – Loxley had been with the United Nations after leaving the army, and Hinton was an ambassador – now advanced in years, conversation tended not to rise much above politics, prices, and the private lives of their neighbours.

Everyone expressed dismay that Violet Tysoe was not well enough to attend the party. 'We'll miss her,' said Sir Geoffrey.

'Indeed. It's a pity too I can never invite Winifred Chadwick to these occasions,' said Sylvia's mother. 'She always spends Christmas at her niece's family home, near Guildford. She lives above on the top floor.' Gertrude pushed her head up towards the ceiling. 'It's a bigger flat than this one. It has three bedrooms as well as a dining-room.' The champagne had loosened her tongue. 'As I told you, my daughter, Sylvia, is here. So we'll be six.'

'Do they have long Christmas holidays in Japan?' asked Mrs Loxley. 'I thought they were Buddhists or Shintoists and would not celebrate Our Lord's birthday.' The Loxleys had been to church that morning.

'I've no idea. I've hardly had the chance to speak to her. She only arrived last night. She telephoned from Tokyo and said she was coming home and—'

Sylvia appeared at the door of the drawing-room with the second bottle of champagne. 'Happy Christmas everyone!' she exclaimed.

The two men rose and reiterated her salutations.

'Oh don't get up,' said Sylvia after they had done so. She greeted the ex-ambassadress and Mrs Loxley, and poured champagne into their empty glasses.

'Lunch is ready when you are,' Sylvia informed her mother.

'I was asking your mother how long a holiday you get at Christmas, which surely can't be a Japanese festival,' said Mrs Loxley.

'No, it isn't, but the New Year is an important holiday. I must be back by January the eighth, that is if I'm going back.'

'Not going back?' In Gertrude's question surprise was mixed with a tinge of alarm.

'Don't you like Tokyo then?' asked Sir Geoffrey. 'I was never *en poste* there, but Molly and I went there on leave from Bangkok, where I was at the embassy. Found it distasteful. Ugliness without relief. The crowds. You didn't like it, did you, darling?' The ex-ambassador regarded his wife.

'Oh, I don't know. The embassy in Tokyo was perfectly all right. We stayed there. The Barratts were more hospitable than some ambassadors and their wives are.'

'Really, Molly!' put in Sir Geoffrey.

Turning to her husband, Lady Hinton said, 'Well perhaps

you've forgotten how mean the Musgroves were in Jakarta.' She looked at Sylvia. 'Anyway, to go back to Japan. I liked Kyoto. The hotel was very comfortable, well-run, the service impeccable, if rather impersonal. Possibly that's why Sylvia is in two minds about going back: the impersonality of the Japanese.'

Still amazed, Gertrude said, 'D'you really mean to say you may not go back to Japan?'

'Yes, Mummy, I may not.'

'Why not?'

'I've been sacked.'

'Sacked!' Gertrude's cry put an end to Sir Geoffrey's further remarks about Japan to Colonel Loxley.

'I'll tell you all about it over lunch, if you like. Shall we go and eat? I've opened both bottles of claret.'

They all rose. Lady Hinton, a bit on her high horse after the champagne, led the way down the passage to the converted bedroom.

'I hope Bernard,' Gertrude said to Colonel Loxley, 'you will carve the bird as usual.'

'Of course, of course.'

'Bernard the great carver,' remarked Sir Geoffrey, somewhat sarcastically, perhaps suggesting he would do it better.

5

The day after Boxing Day saw Barbara Lane, Neville, Jennifer and Peter Cochrane installed in a hotel near the Night Market in Chiang Mai. Having lived in Thailand for nearly ten years, Peter knew the ropes. He had managed to secure Arthit's release from the police station by parting with a fair sum which came from the company's coffers, as would the expenses for Henry's funeral and the Lanes' hotel bills. Peter felt responsible in a mild way for not trying to prevent Henry from going to Chiang Mai from Bangkok in Arthit's truck. He knew of Henry's relationship with the driver and disapproved of it; he thought it was bad for the company to have a director from the London office involved in an affair with one of the junior employees, albeit a good and reliable man, who had not, as far as Peter knew, taken advantage of his connection with Henry.

6

Sydney Street
London NW1

14th January

Dear Leonard,

Thanks for your letter of the 5th Jan., which came today. The Thai post isn't very quick, but that doesn't bother many people, I suspect.

I might well join you in Thailand. It depends on my assistant, Beatrice Cox. I don't like to leave her on her own in the shop for too long and January and February are usually good months for the sale of porcelain. I might fly out for a week at the end of the month on the pretext (to satisfy my own conscience) of buying some Thai ceramics. I should very much like to get hold of some *kalong* plates, the black designs on them are very attractive and there are not many about in London.

The Lanes – Barbara, Neville and Jennifer – back from the funeral in Chiang Mai, are leaving again soon for Thailand. They're quite crazy. There is to be some ceremony in the graveyard: the unveiling of Henry's tombstone; and they want to be present for it. Jennifer, who came to see me in the office last week, told me that Arthit, Henry's Thai lover, was left no less than £50,000, and that the family are furious about it. The richer you are the more you want to have. But there will be plenty.

Henry, she told me, left well over two million, and then there's Grasslands, the family home near Guildford, which was in his wife's name, and the wife has money of her own, a lot, I believe. So the fury about the Thai inheriting so much isn't all that strong, not rage proportions anyway. Jennifer said she'd been left £70,000. She's resigned from the department store in Oxford Street and is going to let her London flat and stay on in Chiang Mai after the ceremony with the idea of living with the Thai art teacher she met with you, apparently.

As far as I know Yuichi Matsumoto, the Japanese painter, is still staying with Barbara's aunt, Jennifer's great aunt, in Hove. Jennifer told me that Yuichi had begun to paint the aunt's portrait.

The reason for Jennifer's visit was to ask me what I thought of her going back to Chiang Mai to live with her Thai boyfriend, who is called Somsak, as you may remember. How could I advise? She of course wanted me to tell her she was doing the right thing. Her mother and brother are opposed to the scheme. It seems that I was about the only person she knew who would listen to her sympathetically. I told her, as you would have done, to do what she thought was wise. She said that such advice was not advice but evasion. Would I please tell her what she should do. So I said, 'go and have a shot at it. You're only young once.' At that, she kissed me and ran out of the shop. 'The impulsive Lanes!' I've heard them called by Veronica, Neville's wife.

You ask if I think you should buy your ex-lover, Trevor, a flat. To this question, I reply, 'Yes'. Or give him enough money to buy one. You can easily afford to do so. I know that.

I'll let you know about my arrival.

    Love,
        Wilson

7

Trevor Hanson, Leonard Crampstead's lover, 'ex' since he flung himself out of Leonard's flat just before Christmas, was beginning to regret his impetuosity. If he hadn't lost his temper when Leonard admitted to bedding down with Yuichi on several occasions, he would now be in Leonard's spacious apartment in Rutland Gate, instead of in his friend Christopher's one-bedroom flat near White City. Trevor had to sleep on the sofa-bed in the sitting-room.

Leonard had taken to spending the winter in Thailand leaving Trevor in charge of the sumptuous establishment crammed with priceless works of art. Trevor felt proud that he was trusted, but there were Mrs Johnson, who had known Leonard far longer than he, and Anacleta, the Filipina maid. The maid didn't count but Mrs Johnson had Leonard's interests at heart. Trevor had often speculated on how much Leonard had left her in his will. He guessed that her loyalty had been bought, with promises, at least. Sensibly, Leonard was continually generous to his cook-housekeeper. Her attitude towards her employer's proclivities was one of indifference – 'it's nothing to do with me what he likes; he's good to me, pays me well' was what she seemed to say. Trevor had never discussed Leonard with Mrs Johnson; he had treated her with respect, playing the difficult role of employer's live-in lover with tact, never taking advantage of his special relationship. Trevor was a mild, easy-going person, not irascible, but Leonard's infidelity with 'that Japanese bisexual bastard' had been too much for him to bear. He had exploded and now he was beginning to wish he hadn't.

And that 'rat Yuichi' was now living with Barbara Lane's aunt in a luxury flat in Hove. Aunt Winifred they called her and she was seventy-five if a day.

Jennifer was lucky to have extricated herself from Yuichi's grasp and all through a misapprehension. When she had peeped into the drawing-room at Grasslands late on Christmas

Eve and seen Trevor and Yuichi rolling about on the floor, she had mistaken the fight for lovemaking and had run off to her flat in London in her car. Yuichi's firm judo hold had surprised Trevor, who had provoked the Japanese by kicking him on the shins and calling him 'a fucking Jap'. The placid Trevor had acted out of character. What was he to do now? He couldn't sponge off his friend Christopher for ever.

8

A few days after Christmas Gertrude Hawkins said to her daughter, 'Sylvia, the caretaker of these flats – Ron we call him – is somewhat of a gossip; he likes to chatter about the tenants; anyway, he told me that a young Japanese artist has come to stay with Winifred Chadwick – I mentioned her to you the other day, on Christmas Day in fact, when the others were here, do you remember?'

'Yes, Mummy.'

'Apparently the Japanese has taken over Mrs Chadwick's companion's room and is using it as a studio. The companion is away at the moment.' Throwing a mischievous regard at her daughter, she added, 'I wonder what will happen when she returns.'

Sylvia made no reply.

'I think I shall ask them in for a drink. Would you like that? You've just come from Japan. The Japanese might be pleased to meet someone who knows his country. What do you think, Sylvia?'

'I don't mind meeting them.'

Sylvia had not tried to contact her ex-husband; she had no desire to see him, but she did wish to see Mark, her son, in spite of her dislike of his lover, Colin Sibley, the actor. Mark was also an actor. Sylvia had seen him act with Sibley. He was Marchbanks to Sibley's Morell in *Candida* and Ariel to Sibley's Prospero in *The Tempest* when Sibley's company were on tour in

Japan. But now they were touring Australia. The London flat in Kensington which came to her as part of the divorce settlement was let, so she had to stay with her mother, with whom she had never got on.

9

Matthew Bennet, who was Sylvia Field's colleague at the university in Tokyo, often felt he should have interceded on Sylvia's behalf when she was told that her contract would not be renewed for a further year. Professor Suzuki, a xenophobe in spite of his being a teacher of English, had successfully intrigued to bring down Sylvia because she had rebuffed him. All he had done was to look into her eyes and place a hand on her knee and she had frowned and quickly risen; after all she had invited him to dinner in her flat and plied him with drinks. What did she expect? Suzuki had been absurdly put out by Sylvia's abrupt rejection of his mild advance. But the Japanese was intensely proud and had felt that she considered herself superior to him, and this rankled. What irked Suzuki even more was the fact that she had taken on a young Japanese bank clerk as her lover. That she preferred Toshi, an ignorant stripling, to him, in his own eyes a sophisticated intellectual, was more than the professor could tolerate. Patiently, like a lizard waiting to catch an insect, he had waited, and seeing an opportunity had sought his revenge and won it. His lost face was recovered.

Matthew suffered qualms of guilt when he thought about the unfair dismissal. He had not backed Sylvia by accompanying her, as she had requested, when she had appealed to the president of the university. Throughout his years of teaching in Japan he had never been sure if his two-year contract would be renewed. He had now been granted tenure, but he supposed it could always be withdrawn; the authorities could no doubt find an excuse to do so if they wanted to. And when Sylvia's brush with the university had arisen he had been too pusillanimous to stick out his neck and openly support her; he could not bring himself to be honourable enough to resign when her contract was cancelled. Foreign teachers were on sufferance in a way; at least they felt they were.

Matthew's other problem was Jun Sakamoto, his lover. He did not doubt Jun's affection for him, but he could not expect his loyalty to him to be stronger than that which he owed his parents. The pressure for Jun to get married, he was twenty-nine, increased every year. So far Jun had managed to refuse the girls provided by his mother as prospective spouses. After each engagement meeting Jun had invented grounds for rejecting a suggested bride, but it was becoming more and more difficult to defy the wishes of his parents. He was the only son and to conform with the customs of Japanese society and to provide grandchildren (especially a son) for his father and mother was in their eyes his duty. Jun couldn't tell his parents that he would find a fiancée on his own and not expect them to find one for him, as he didn't know any girls, and didn't want to. At the school where he taught English there wasn't one female colleague he could possibly consider marrying. Neither could he tell his parents he was gay. They simply wouldn't understand.

Recently in the Japanese press and on television there had been much reference to male and female homosexuality. The gay men had usually been represented by screaming queens in drag who camped it up in a manner that made them appear freaks. Jun feared that if he confessed to his parents his true tastes they would assume that he was like one of those creatures who wanted to have their genitals amputated. The average middle-class Japanese, especially those who lived in the provinces, imagined that a gay meant a hopelessly effeminate man, a sister-boy. In many cities there were sister-boy bars staffed by men, young and old, dressed like geishas or hostesses in Western dresses. The clientele of such places were mostly straight men who found the exaggerated antics and the risqué banter of the 'girls' amusing.

Jun could not possibly admit to his parents that he was a 'homo', a pejorative for gays in Japan. His mother would be overcome with shame; his father might disown him and blame his wife for giving birth to a monster. Jun could not be the cause of such distress in his family.

Matthew knew all this, of course, and didn't like to object too strongly when Jun had an engagement meeting; he did hope, though, that it would come to nothing; and so far each such meeting had. Matthew was so happy with Jun. The sexual side of the relationship, which had once been as torrid as a typhoon, had slowly moved into the doldrums and become unimportant. At the beginning of their affair sex had sealed their liaison, now something stronger had taken its place: a deep love. Matthew prayed that the affair would continue. He could not expect it to last forever, but each year he said to himself, 'Just a little longer, please.'

Matthew, then, had two worries: the cancellation of his tenure and Jun being forced into marriage.

10

'I no want to go,' said Yuichi Matsumoto to the septuagenarian Winifred Chadwick, who had taken him under her wing.

'Oh, you must.' Winifred was firm. 'Mrs Hawkins's daughter is back from Japan. She wants to meet you.'

'How she know about me?'

'She knows no more than the fact that you are here looking after me while . . .' Winifred stopped herself from adding 'while Miss Pinnock is away'. She had not thought of what she was going to do when the housekeeper returned from her Christmas holiday; throughout her easy life she had put distasteful, imminent dilemmas out of her mind until the last moment, and then she acted on instinct.

'What I wear?' asked Yuichi, who had on a yellow polo sweater and blue jeans.

'You look perfectly all right as you are, Yuichi. Come, let us go.'

'You not wear your wig. Please wear.'

'Why? You know I only put it on when you are painting my portrait. And I must wear a hat.'

'You wear wig for surprise, Wicku-san.' Yuichi laughed and so did Winifred, who liked his merry chortle.

'Why you wear hat?'

'It is polite to do so when one old lady visits another.'

'We not go out, jus' downstair.'

'It's as if we were going to another house. All right, I'll wear the wig but I'll put my hat over it.'

Before they left the flat Yuichi curled a few strands of the russet wig over the brim of Winifred's brown felt hat giving a coquettish touch to the old lady's appearance. 'I think I'll wear my fur coat, Yuichi.'

'We go down one floor only.'

'It's so draughty in the passage. We may have to wait for the lift.' Winifred liked to wear her mink coat, but rarely did so as she had been told that if she went out in it she might have it stripped off her by the Animal Rights Group. 'It's not as if I myself had killed the wretched little animals which, I believe, are as fierce and destructive as rats,' she would say.

11

Barbara always referred to her son's flat in Kensington as 'Neville's'. 'I'm going to Neville's', she would say to her late husband, Henry. It was too much of a mouthful to say 'Neville's and Veronica's'. Over dinner at 'Neville's', Veronica, Barbara's daughter-in-law, said, 'I really don't see the point of you all going to Chiang Mai for the unveiling, or whatever you call it, of Henry's headstone. Surely the representative of Henry's company –'

'Peter Cochrane,' put in Neville.

'Surely,' went on Veronica, 'he could send you a photograph.'

Barbara, who wanted to go to Chiang Mai to have another flirtation with Jim, the Thai barman, said, 'I simply must go. I won't feel that Henry's been properly buried until I see the stone in place.'

'I have to go,' said Jennifer excitedly. 'I've resigned from the store, as you know, and I'm in love. I want to see the stone, of course, but I also want desperately to see Somsak. I'm in love with Somsak, don't you realise that?'

'Someone you've only known for a few days.' Veronica, who disliked Jennifer, sneered.

'Yes,' Jennifer replied fiercely. 'It doesn't take any time to fall in love. It happens at once, didn't you know?'

'You haven't heard from him, darling,' said Barbara.

'You don't expect an illiterate Thai to write letters,' remarked Neville.

Jennifer stormed, 'He's not illiterate. He teaches at a school. He has a degree from an art college in Bangkok. He has a photograph of himself receiving his degree from the King.'

'I'm sorry,' replied Neville, who was fond of his sister. He tried to appease Jennifer's anger by adding, 'Artists often aren't very good letter writers. Why don't you telephone him or rather why doesn't he phone you?'

'He hasn't a phone, and it's impossible for him to phone abroad from the school.'

Veronica rose and collected the plates off which the family quartet had eaten mushrooms *à la Greque*, an easy dish to make and one which Neville liked, even though she had served it cold. It was Wednesday and she had given two lectures that morning at the London college where she worked. Neville half rose when Veronica reached his place. 'No, darling. I can manage. I wish you weren't going to Thailand,' she murmured.

'But I must go,' answered Neville in a voice that everyone could hear. 'I'm his only son. I'll not be away for more than a week; that's all the bank can give me anyway.' Ever since his return from his father's funeral in Chiang Mai he had called to mind, particularly when he was lying next to his lanky wife in bed, the willing, thrilling lively smooth brown body of the lithe Thai girl he had made love to in that sordid room above a café. She had drugged him and taken the money out of his wallet; nevertheless, he longed to have her or someone like her again. If he were honest with himself he would admit that he was really going to Thailand in the hope of finding another girl like Noi, even though she was a thief, and not for the unveiling of his father's headstone in the little foreigners' cemetery.

'Wilson Gill is going to Chiang Mai,' said Veronica. 'Or he may have gone there by now. He was joining Leonard Crampstead. They are great friends.'

'I liked Leonard,' said Barbara.

'So did I, really,' echoed Jennifer.

'Silly old poof,' muttered Neville.

'And what about Daddy?' asked his sister.

This remark brought about an awkward silence. Veronica took the plates to the kitchen; after a pause, Neville rose with noticeable reluctance and joined his wife.

'Jennifer, you shouldn't have said that.'

'But Mummy it's true. We must face facts.'

'It's hurtful to me to do so.'

'I'm sorry. Mummy, I'm longing to see Somsak.'

'I know you are, darling. But you must be sensible about him. You hardly know him.'

'I know my future lies with him.'

'And what about Yuichi?' Barbara blushed when she mentioned the name of the Japanese.

'He's just a promiscuous satyr. He'll go to bed with anyone.'

Barbara, feeling guilty about her own indiscretion with Yuichi, changed the subject. 'I wonder what Veronica is giving us next.'

The kitchen door swung open and Neville entered with a roast chicken on a platter.

'Oh,' uttered Barbara on a falling tone of disappointment. 'Cecily gave me chicken for lunch.'

12

'Why didn't you tell me before?' asked Matthew of Jun. It was after the Christmas party. They had done the washing-up together, cheerfully discussing the party and their guests while they did so; now they were in their separate beds in the bedroom. The lights were out.

'I didn't want to spoil the party. I knew you'd be upset.' There was a tremor in Jun's voice.

'Must you go through with it, Jun?'

'Yes, I must. She is not so bad. I quite liked her. She's twenty-four, also a teacher. Not "wickie".'

Matthew snorted; he usually laughed at Jun's version of 'wicked'. 'I should hope not. Will you be able to fuck her?'

'I shall try,' replied Jun, seriously. 'You know, Mattu-san, my parents have only one son – me. I must marry, give them a grandson. Don't you understand?'

'Only too well do I know the strict conventions of the Japanese middle-class. It's about time they were broken.'

'I cannot disobey to my parents, Mattu-san. I owe everything to them.'

'And what about me? Do you owe nothing to me?'

'Of course I owe everything to you too, but . . .'

'But what?'

'You are not my father.'

'I am your lover. Does that count for nothing?'

'I can go on seeing you. I promise I'll see you once a week, one night a week.'

'That'll be rather different from living with me.'

'I cannot help it, Mattu-san. Maybe twice a week.' Jun

stretched out an arm and with his hand tapped Matthew's bedclothes; it was a sign that he wanted Matthew to hold his hand and to make up a disagreement or to reconfirm their affection for each other. In response Matthew turned on his right side, his back to the pleading hand.

13

Sylvia opened the door to Winifred and Yuichi. 'Mrs Chadwick? I'm Sylvia Field, Gertrude's daughter.'

'How do you do? This is Yuichi Matsumoto.'

'I'll lead the way, but please take off your coat. Let me help you.' The old lady shed her heavy fur coat with Sylvia's help. 'Gertrude's in the drawing-room.'

Gertrude kissed Winifred on her thickly powdered cheek and shook hands with Yuichi, who muttered his name.

'Now, what will you drink?' asked Sylvia.

Gertrude, eyeing Winifred's red curls, said, 'Do sit down.'

'Thank you. May I have a gin and lime? I know it's old-fashioned, but I feel like a gin and lime today. My husband and I often drank gin and lime.'

Yuichi asked for a gin and tonic.

When the little group were seated and supplied with drinks, the conversation, led by Gertrude, was general for a while. Soon the two old ladies were exchanging views about the flats and their occupants, and Sylvia talked to Yuichi, whom she found agreeable; his stay in England had rid him of that irritating shyness inherent in so many Japanese. She gave her impressions of Tokyo omitting to mention Toshi and the fact that the university had terminated her contract; Yuichi praised life in England failing to mention his affair with Jennifer and his weekly meetings with Leonard Crampstead. They touched on the advantages and disadvantages of living in both countries. Sylvia extolling Japan, Yuichi England. Sylvia was attracted by Yuichi's Japanese looks and his Japanese accent; he made her think of Toshi and realise how much she missed her lover – there was no Toshi in England. Yuichi's presence, his smile, his dark eyes, succeeded in swaying Sylvia's uncertain mind in favour of returning to Tokyo.

Two days later Sylvia rang for the lift and when she stepped into it there was Yuichi.

Sylvia greeted the young Japanese by saying, '*Konichi-wa* – good afternoon.'

'*Konichi-wa*,' he responded. 'You know Japanese?'

'As I told you, I know only a few words.'

'You go shopping?' Yuichi's English was far from perfect, but his manner of speaking was full of charm.

'Yes. And you?'

It was a cold January day, blustery and drizzly. They both wore raincoats, Yuichi a very short one. Sylvia's head was wreathed in a silk scarf, and Yuichi was wearing a deerstalker hat which didn't suit his pale, delicate face; it was an incongruous as a hat on a kitten, a sort of joke.

'Where did you get that hat?'

'I like. I buy. Sherlock Holmes.'

'You read Conan Doyle?'

'Uh?'

Sylvia presumed he had seen the TV films. She wondered if Toshi had heard of the famous sleuth. Yuichi again made her think of Toshi. In spite of the reconciliation after their quarrel, or rather their misunderstanding, there remained an uncertainty. He had lied, but then so had she.

Sylvia and Yuichi purchased their supplies at the same store in Church Road. 'It's stopped raining, Yuichi. Let's go back by the sea.'

Each with a plastic carrier bag (Yuichi did not offer to carry hers) they made their way to the sea front. They had to shout to make themselves heard above the crash of the waves, the jangle of the pebbles, the wind. 'How long will you stay in England?' asked Sylvia.

'I don't know. I will study at art school in Blighton soon.'
'Where?'
'In Blighton.'
'Let's sit in that shelter.'

They sat out of the wind and could hear one another. A bent old woman dragging an unwilling Yorkshire terrier passed by.

'The English and their dogs,' Sylvia remarked with distaste.
'You no like dog?'
'In the country they are fine. Not in a town messing up the pavements. Do you like it here?'
'Wicku-san she very kind to me.'
'Who?'
'Mrs Chadwick. I call her Wicku-san.'
'How sweet!' said Sylvia, thinking of how Toshi had changed her name to 'Siru-san'.

They sat in silence for a while. Sylvia thought of Toshi and wished he was as sophisticated as Yuichi seemed to be; and then after exchanging views about living in their countries they told each other about their affairs in Tokyo and London. Yuichi was surprisingly frank about his sexual exploits.

14

'I moved to this hotel, the Golden Plaza,' Leonard explained to Wilson Gill after they had got into the minibus at the Chiang Mai airport, 'because the Lanes are due back.'

'It was good of you to meet me.'

'The hotel bus is free, or I think it is. I don't want to get mixed up with the Lanes. They are having a peculiar ceremony for the unveiling of the husband's headstone.'

'I heard all about that; in fact it was I who told you about it in my letter.'

'Of course it was. How gaga I'm getting. I had thought of going to Chiang Rai, but it's such a dull town. I chose the

Golden Plaza – what a name – because it's a little way out of the centre. It has a good pool.'

There were no other guests to collect so the driver put the hotel placard which he had been holding up to attract would-be customers in the back of the bus, and they set off.

'I knew Henry Lane well,' said Wilson smoothing his thick white hair with a hand. 'We used to meet once in a while to have sessions.'

'Sessions?'

'Film sessions. Porn. Soft, mostly.'

'You never told me. You are a secretive old devil.'

The bus approached the corner of the south-west wall of the old moated city – Chiang Mai now sprawled well beyond its original confines.

'This place has grown,' said Wilson.

'Like everywhere. Nowhere improves.'

'Nor do we.'

They turned west away from the moat and joined a pot-holed road which took them past the hospital. In front of one of the buildings a statue of the King's father stood on a stepped pedestal.

'He was a doctor, you know,' said Leonard.

'I did know. He made the Thai medical profession a respected one. This isn't my first visit to Chiang Mai.'

They bumped along and then turned right. The experimental farm of Chiang Mai University was on the left, a green plantation; on the right was a new building with a ponderous pointed roof over the entrance.

'What's that?' asked Wilson.

'Some centre, I think, for functions. The Thais are fond of functions, which become parties. They love *sanuk* – fun.' Leonard had a penchant for imparting information, even to an old hand.

In front of the modern erection a formal garden with young trees in rows was being laid out; then came a park in which there was a gazebo, a shelter with a seat and table covered by a quadrangular roof on a little hillock; it had a sort of Chinese look, one could imagine a seated sage meditating there.

'Fitness Park,' Leonard announced. 'In the early mornings and in the evenings it's full of joggers. Students mostly.'

'Do you jog with them?'

'No. I sometimes go for a stroll.'

In view was a number of high-rise blocks: apartments and hotels.

'This place has grown upwards as well as outwards,' remarked Wilson.

'The apartment blocks are often money-laundering operations,' said Leonard. 'That's a good Thai restaurant,' he went on, pointing to an old Thai house half-hidden among trees. 'I often go there. It has a very good headwaiter.'

'By good, do you mean good-looking?'

'No, no,' protested Leonard. 'He knows his job. Does it well.'

The bus pulled up at the hotel entrance. Two bellboys in dark blue uniforms hurried out to take Wilson's bags, and the friends mounted the steps into the lobby and approached the front desk, where a pretty, smiling Thai girl gave Wilson a registration form to fill in and a magenta-coloured drink with a straw sticking out of the glass. 'Your room is next to mine,' said Leonard. 'We overlook the pool.'

Wilson sucked up a little of the magenta liquid and made a face.

The room keys were handed to the bellboy, who had put the bags on a trolley, and the two old men followed the boy down a long passage.

'I expect you'd like a rest,' said Leonard to Wilson.

'I'd like something to eat. The food on both planes, the one from London and the one from Bangkok, looked unappetising so I didn't have any. I didn't have a drink either. They say one suffers less from jet lag if one fasts.'

'What nonsense! And there are those pills you can take to

accustom your body to the time change. We can go up to the coffee shop. I thought that tonight, if you feel up to it, we might pay a little visit to "My Cup".'

'"My Cup"? What on earth is that?'

Leonard lowered his voice. 'A gay bar. I suppose they got the name from "My cup of tea", so at "My Cup" you meet your "cup".'

'Gayese is marvellously ungrammatical. What about "He isn't me"?'

'But,' replied Leonard, '"he" may turn out to be "you" at "My Cup".'

Chuckling, the couple entered the lift, whose door the bellboy was holding open for them. When they reached the bedroom Wilson pulled out a twenty *baht* note from his wallet and started to hand it to the bellboy.

'Oh, give him a hundred,' commanded Leonard.

'A hundred?' Wilson frowned and reluctantly did so.

The bellboy beamed and left the room after making a *wai* with a pink banknote between his fingers.

'A hundred was rather a lot, wasn't it?' objected Wilson. 'It's over two pounds.'

'One should always start off with a good impression when one arrives at a place.'

15

'I can't think why you're going,' said Veronica to her husband, who was about to depart for Thailand. 'Of all the unnecessary trips this one beats them all.'

'I can't let mother go on her own,' replied Neville. 'She attaches so much importance to seeing the stone in place.'

'Jennifer will be with her,' Veronica reminded Neville.

'She's too besotted with her Thai artist to be of much help. I'll only be away a week.'

'There's the baby.'

'You can have the nurse sleep in the spare room while I'm away.'

'And Jennifer, will she stay on in Chiang Mai?'

'I've no idea. You know how headstrong she is.' He looked at his watch. 'I'd better go now, darling.' He kissed his wife on the cheek and hurried out of the flat.

16

Barbara and Jennifer were waiting at Cecily's house for Neville to pick them up and take them to Heathrow, where he was going to park his car during his week of absence. They had spent the night with Cecily having been driven up on the previous afternoon from Grasslands by Barbara's gardener, who lived with his wife in a bungalow by the gate.

'I can't wait to go,' said Jennifer. 'I do wish Neville would come.'

'We've plenty of time,' replied her mother.

'To me it seems the maddest escapade,' remarked Cecily, an old family friend who had been at school with Barbara. 'To go all that way for a week and just to see a grave.'

'You wouldn't say that if you had married and lost you husband in a tragic accident,' snapped Barbara. 'His life was cut off in its prime,' she added in a melodramatic tone.

'A husband who was unfaithful with a—' began Cecily.

'Whatever he might have done he was my husband and I loved him,' interrupted Barbara.

'Neville's here,' cried Jennifer from the window, her voice quivering with excitement like that of a child half her age – she was twenty-four.

17

'I don't think he'll be here very long, Miss Pinnock,' said Winifred to her housekeeper, who had just returned from her

Christmas holiday. 'You could go back to your sister at Diss until he leaves, if you like.'

'He's made a mess of my room, piled my family photographs anyhow in a corner, covered my bed with his painting things and he's created chaos in the kitchen. The sink is full of unwashed-up dishes. He's taken over the spare room too. Where am I to sleep, pray? I wish to give you notice, Mrs Chadwick, from now, this moment.'

'Oh, don't do that, Miss Pinnock.' It was just what Winifred wanted her to do. She much preferred Yuichi's company, even though she knew it had to be temporary, to that of the dull, insipid, uninspiring Miss Pinnock. Yuichi's English was limited, but he did come out with remarks that amused and sometimes startled her: also, he made her do things, like eating in the kitchen with him, taking her for little walks by the sea, which was only two hundred yards away, and making her pose for her portrait; he made her feel younger, and, what's more, wanted. Miss Pinnock would grouse and, Winifred had to admit, Yuichi could sulk, but never for long, and he was young and lively, and interesting because he was different.

'Well then, Miss Pinnock, if you feel you must go, you must go.'

'There's no room for me here any more.'

'I'm sure Mr Yuichi would move his painting paraphernalia out of your room for a night or two while you get your things together. I'll miss you, you know.' That last statement lacked any ring of sincerity.

'I always did my best for you, Mrs Chadwick.' The housekeeper became tearful.

'And I shall always be grateful. You can now go to that sister of yours at Diss. You've often said she wanted you to live with her.'

'I'm not so sure she does now. I think we saw enough of each other over Christmas.' Miss Pinnock sniffed, and swallowed a sob. 'Where am I to go? I mean at this moment.'

'Mr Yuichi will be back from his art school soon, and you can move into your old room, but don't touch his painting things. Let him do that.'

'I'm not going to wash up his mess in the kitchen.'

'It's partly my mess, you know.' Winifred gave a watery smile.

'I used to regard this place as my home,' wailed Miss Pinnock as she began to leave the sitting-room. 'Now I've nowhere to go.'

'I'll see you're all right,' said Winifred.

At the threshold the housekeeper turned and looked back at her employer. 'All right? What does that mean?'

'It means what it usually means,' replied the old lady firmly and without emotion; it suddenly came to Winifred that she wouldn't have to pay Yuichi a salary, only provide for his keep.

Miss Pinnock turned again and went down the passage and met Yuichi, who had just entered the flat. He gave her a curt bow, announced his name and still in his raincoat and wearing his deerstalker hat went down the passage to the drawing-room, where Winifred was now perusing the *Evening Argus*.

'There's never anything of interest in this paper,' Winifred complained to herself. 'When Pinnock goes I shall stop it.'

'Haro!'

The old lady looked up. 'Yuichi, dear, you ought to take off your hat when you come indoors, and your coat too when you come in here.' Yuichi quickly shed his outer coverings. 'Miss Pinnock is here. Did you see her? She will only stay a day or two. She must sleep in her room, so will you please move your painting things into the spare room.'

'Maybe I go.'

'Go? Where? What do you mean?'

'Maybe it better I reave and Pinnock-san she stay.'

'No, no, no, Yuichi. I want you to stay. You can't possibly leave. You haven't finished my portrait.' Winifred realised it had been rash to get rid of her housekeeper, but she was infatuated with the young Japanese and could not bear the thought of his going. Miss Pinnock had been engaged as a companion-help – Winifred's niece, Barbara, had told her that the word servant was obsolete – but she had not proved to be much of a companion, and her cooking lacked imagination. Winifred hated sitting with her at meals in the dining-room, usually in silence; conversation with her was limited; the only subjects they had in common were the weather, the shops, prices, church, some of the parishioners and the other occupants of the flats. Miss Pinnock regularly attended the Sung Eucharist on Sundays; Winifred sometimes did. Winifred denied Miss Pinnock her manifest desire to know more about the doings of the Lane family: Jennifer's latest affair, Henry's scandalous behaviour in Thailand, Barbara's lapse with Yuichi, for example – the last indiscretion Winifred herself didn't know of, though her niece had eulogised Yuichi to her on a visit to Hove. With the young Japanese it was different; she felt such a strong affinity towards him that she could confide in him almost completely, almost, because she strictly excluded finance from the topics that could be discussed in spite of the fact that it was a topic that was constantly on her mind, but he never inquired about her money matters and never referred to the long conversations she had on the phone with her financial adviser. Unlike many of the modern young, Yuichi didn't treat her as if she were a fossil, a thing to be ignored, an object in the way. He behaved towards her with respect, not with awe, regarding her more like an elder sister than a tiresome crone.

18

'She's back!' cried Matthew as he entered the flat. The cry went unanswered since Jun was out. As soon as Matthew heard Jun's key in the lock and the door bursting open he cried out again, 'You were wrong.'

'What d'you mean?'

'She's back.'

'Oh?'

'She told me she wanted to finish her contract.'

'But they cancel her contract.'

'Finish the academic year then. And she's taking up the job she was offered in that publishing company.'

Jun uttered his sceptical 'Huh!' and went into the kitchen to have a snack before supper. It was past six o'clock and he was hungry. He went along with Matthew's insistence on not dining till eight, but he needed some sustenance at the Japanese hour for the evening meal.

19

Unbeknown to him, it was Yuichi who caused Sylvia's return to Tokyo – Yuichi and her mother. A week in the Hove flat had been enough to make her realise that she could not possibly live with her parent. She would disrupt the bridge, the dinner parties with the 'old fogies' and the shopping expeditions to a supermarket in her Mini, which her mother drove in a vague manner; and didn't like criticism, something which Sylvia couldn't resist. During the bridge parties there was nowhere for Sylvia to escape to except for the cubby-hole of a spare room, where there wasn't even enough space for an armchair. Sylvia felt *de trop* in her mother's flat. There was no other refuge in England. Her own London flat was let, and she couldn't seek shelter in the apartment that Mark, her only child, shared with Colin Sibley, his lover. They were abroad anyway. Her chance meeting with Yuichi had, more than anything, made her decide to return to Japan. He revived memories of the Japan that fascinated her; of Toshi who, when they were reunited, had thrown himself into her arms and declared his undying love. Yuichi reminded her of the charms of Toshi and made her decide to take the return flight to Tokyo, which she had already booked.

The first thing she did when she arrived back in her Tokyo apartment was telephone Matthew. It was around noon, and he was in.

'Jun was sure you wouldn't come back,' he said. 'I was sure you would.'

'I was in two minds about returning myself, and nearly didn't. I felt I should finish the academic year properly in spite of my dismissal, and—' she paused.

'And what? Toshi?'

'Yes. Toshi. How did you guess?'

'You put finishing your job honourably as your first reason, when really you should have put Toshi first. It's the Toshis that bring us back to Japan or make us stay, not our half-understood performances in the classroom.'

'You sound a bit down, Matthew. Are you?'

'Decidedly so. Jun has got engaged.'

'It was bound to happen, wasn't it?'

'Yes, but I hoped it wouldn't. I've half a mind to resign from the university.'

'I wish I could ring Toshi at the bank.'

'You know his family name?'

'Yes, Yamada.'

'Then ring the bank and ask for him. Say Yamada Toshihiko-san. He's in the foreign department, isn't he? So it would be perfectly in order to ring him at the bank and ask for him. See you at the university tomorrow, then.'

Sylvia, heart racing, hands trembling, dialled the number of the branch of the Four Square Bank, and asked for her lover. 'Yamada Toshihiko-san, *kudasai*,' she said, her voice unsteady. She got through at once.

'Is that Yamada-san?'

'Mrs Field? What can I do for you?' His tone was impersonal, that of the busy banker. She knew he was in a room containing several other employees of the Foreign Section, one of them probably breathing down his neck.

'Six-thirty,' she said, 'can you?'
'Traveller cheque? How many?'
'No. A draft to send to England.'
'How much, please?'
'Sixty and thirty thousand yen. OK?'
'Two draft? One sixty, the other thirty?'
'Yes. Six-thirty, OK?'
'OK. I prepare for you, Mrs Field. Same address as last time?' There was no emotion in his voice. He might easily be taking a genuine order for drafts. She had sent money to Mark before. She put down the phone. Would he come at six-thirty?

20

'We paid all that money to go first class and as soon as we have landed we're no better off than those in economy,' complained Barbara to her son and daughter. They were standing in one of the long and snail-crawling queues in front of the Immigration passport-check desks at Don Muang airport, Bangkok. The Thai officials took their time. Why should they hurry? 'First class ought to include privileged service here,' went on Barbara. 'We should be put at the head of the queue. This waiting and inching along with our hand luggage is a disgrace. Why don't they open more check points, whatever you call them? This is the most tiring part of the flight. I wish I hadn't eaten all that breakfast. It lies heavy.'

'Oh, shut up Mummy,' said Jennifer. 'Scenes are not appreciated in the East. One doesn't complain, one accepts. Isn't that so, Neville?'

'Where did you learn that?'

'Wilson told me.'

'Oh, Wilson,' Neville uttered in a derogatory tone, and changing the subject said, 'I hope Cochrane will meet us. He said he would. He also said something about driving up to Chiang Mai.'

'I don't fancy a long drive after that knock-out flight,' said Barbara.

'He suggested it would be useful to have transport in Chiang Mai.'

'We could hire a car, couldn't we?' said the mother.

'Will Daddy's lover be there?'

'Bound to be,' replied Neville.

'I shan't speak to him,' warned Jennifer.

'I shall,' said Barbara. 'I've had second thoughts about him. I quite liked him in a way. I'm sure he was sincerely devoted to your father. In a seduction it's fifty-fifty, unless it's rape, and it certainly wasn't that. One doesn't leave fifty thousand pounds to one's rapist.'

'You might to your blackmailer,' suggested Jennifer.

Barbara's loud, imperious 'Oh hurry up, for God's sake!' was heard by the bemedalled Immigration official, who raised his eyes from the passport he was examining and glared; he put down his chop and began a conversation with his colleague at the next desk.

21

'"My Cup",' said Leonard to the *tuk-tuk* driver. '*Tao rai*? How much?'

'Two hundred.' The driver was handsome and had a captivating smile with a touch of mischief in it.

Leonard and Wilson were leaning back bulkily side by side in the motorcycle taxi outside the Golden Plaza. 'One hundred baht,' said Leonard.

The driver gave a mocking laugh. 'Very far.'

'Not far. One hundred.'

'OK, one fifty.'

Leonard moved to alight, easing his bottom on to the edge of the seat.

'Are we to get out?' asked Wilson, plaintively.

'One hundred,' insisted Leonard.

'One fifty.'

'No.' Leonard started to heave himself off the seat. 'Get out,' he said to Wilson, as he descended from the machine.

'Oh Lord, must I? It was such a business getting in.' With a groan Wilson struggled to the ground.

'OK,' agreed the driver, ungraciously, his Thai charm evaporated, 'one hundred.'

'Get in,' Leonard commanded Wilson.

Emitting grunts, 'oh dears', 'this damned contraption' (from Wilson), and 'Oh to be young and nimble' (from Leonard), the two old men clambered back into the three-wheeled vehicle. The two-stroke engine roared into action, and off they hurtled down Huey Kaew Road towards the centre of the city, passing, on one side or the other, most of the vehicles going in the same direction.

'Why don't they have taxis,' shouted Wilson to his friend, 'like in Bangkok?'

'They do. Hotel taxis. Fiendishly expensive.'

'Is there no other form of transport?'

'There are infrequent buses, and red vans with bench seats down each side. One has to share them with other passengers, and they often go a roundabout way to drop them off; the roof of the little private buses is so low one has to sit doubled up.'

'I can't think why you don't have a car and a driver at your disposal.'

'Far beyond my pocket.'

They had reached the moat of the ancient city where part of the brick battlements remained; it was illuminated.

'At least they've preserved that,' said Wilson.

The *tuk-tuk* spluttered away at a traffic light confirming its onomatopoeic name. They came to the north-eastern corner of the moat where there was another remnant of fortification, also faintly lit. The *tuk-tuk* left the busy road by the moat and sped up a dark street at the end of which was a *chedi*, and the River

Ping; the driver threaded his way past the cars and trucks through the lines of traffic. They crossed Nawarat Bridge and shot up another dark street of shuttered shop-houses.

It was after ten o'clock when they arrived at "My Cup", a Thai style house in a murky lane. The driver's charm revived when Leonard gave him a hundred *baht* note.

The house stood among coconut palms and mango trees.

'Shoes off,' instructed Leonard. 'Thai customs here.'

'Oh Lord!' muttered Wilson.

In their socks they mounted a few steps and entered a large room whose floor of polished teak was strewn with cushions. Immediately they were surrounded by a cluster of smiling Thai boys eager to serve and entertain.

22

'He's gone to the art school,' said Winifred in reply to Gertrude Hawkins's inquiry about Yuichi. 'How is your daughter getting on now she's back in Tokyo?'

They were having lunch together in the dining-room of Gertrude's flat. Winifred was without her wig and she wore no hat. Gertrude had roasted a chicken; unlike her guest, she enjoyed cooking.

'She's left the university and is working for a publishing company. I don't quite understand what happened in Tokyo,' went on Gertrude. 'She was dismissed from the university.'

'Dismissed?' Winifred successfully put a good measure of astonishment into the word in spite of the fact that Sylvia had told the story to Yuichi, who had related it to her.

'Knife? Why did she go back?'

'She had to finish the academic year and this editing job came up. Would you like to have some more chicken?'

'Oh, no thank you,' replied Winifred.

'A little more wine?'

'Just a little, perhaps. I'm not supposed to have any. Miss

Pinnock, my companion, or I should say my ex-companion, was very strict with me and wouldn't let me have more than one glass. Yuichi gives me tumblers full. Besides, I read recently that wine, especially red wine, was good for the heart. And this is red.' She raised her glass, which Gertrude had replenished. 'Here's luck again!'

Mrs Hawkins toasted her in return. 'Are you pleased to be rid of Miss Pinnock?'

'Yes. I couldn't have them both, now could I? And Yuichi is infinitely more interesting. I was so bored with Pinnock.'

'What will you do when Yuichi leaves? He can't stay here forever, presumably.'

'I don't know. I'm living in the present. Yuichi has made me feel ten years younger.' Winifred drained her glass and pushed it towards the decanter. Gertrude obeyed the silent request.

'What's his history?' she asked Winifred.

'I don't know much about him, really. He came into my life over last Christmas, which I was spending as usual at Grasslands, my niece's place. It was a most dramatic lunch. Right in the middle of the meal the phone rang – one of those cordless things was on the table by Neville – he's Barbara's son – and we learned that Barbara's husband had been killed in a motor accident. His driver, who went smack into a tree, was not hurt at all. And . . .' Winifred leant forward over the table. 'And do you know. The driver was Henry's – Barbara's husband was called Henry – he was Henry's . . .' she dropped her voice to a whisper, 'catamite.'

'Good heavens!'

'Barbara told me when she got home.'

'Would you like some cheese?'

'No, thank you. Well, perhaps a little.'

Gertrude removed the plates, put a platter containing various cheeses on the table and poured some more wine into Winifred's glass. 'I shouldn't, you know,' said the old lady, coyly.

'Ah, there's some *chèvre*, my favourite.' She helped herself to half the little round of goat's cheese.

'So the wife knew?' said Gertrude.

'She learned about it when she got to Thailand. She was on holiday in Egypt at the time of the accident, and she flew straight from Cairo to Bangkok when the news reached her.'

'A tragedy. How old was he?'

'Henry? Well over sixty.'

'And how does Yuichi come into the story?'

'He was Jennifer's boyfriend – she's Barbara's daughter and that girl has had a series of boyfriends. Jennifer and Yuichi had a row, over what I don't know. The upshot of it was that Jennifer left Grasslands in the middle of the night on Christmas Eve, so Yuichi, who had been living with Jennifer had nowhere to go. They had only gone down to Grasslands to spend Christmas with the family. Barbara being away, Veronica, Neville's wife, acted as the hostess. So I took him in.'

'Good of you.'

'Wasn't it!' Winifred put some cheese on a water biscuit. 'There's a mysterious man in the background of the picture. Very rich, apparently. For some reason he helped Yuichi get a student's visa. Jennifer met Yuichi at a party given by this person. His name is Leonard something. Yuichi refers to him as Renardo-san – isn't that sweet? – but says little about him.' Winifred's eyelids fell over her eyes momentarily. 'When I ask Yuichi about him he evades my question in that oriental way of his. I find this irritating but at the same time intriguing.' Again the old eyes closed and the head jerked downwards. With a struggle she continued. 'And Barbara Lane was fascinated by Yuichi too. She . . .' Winifred's chin sank on to her chest and she emitted a snort.

Gertrude did not disturb her. She rose from the table, loaded a tray and took the debris of the meal into the kitchen.

23

'How good of you to meet us,' cried Barbara in her garden-party voice to Peter Cochrane. He was standing among the milling crowd of welcomers penned behind a barrier. Peter's blond head towered about the Thai black ones.

Peter shook hands with the Lane contingent. Neville, also tall, reached over the luggage trolley he was pushing to do so. Arthit, the lover of Barbara's late husband, appeared out of the crowd as suddenly as Ariel, presented himself and took over the trolley, which Neville with an 'oh thanks' let him do. Jennifer gave the Thai a perfunctory 'Hello', but Barbara greeted him warmly, almost gushingly, to the obvious distaste of her children. 'How good to see you!' she cooed to her husband's paramour, squeezing his hand. Arthit and Peter's driver, who had been hovering in the background, went off to the car park to bring their vehicles to where the party was now gathered with the luggage outside the arrival part of the airport.

'Now,' announced Peter. 'I have my car, but it will only take two with my driver and me.'

Neville and Jennifer gave each other a questioning look and then turned their eyes on to Peter, who seemed to guess what they were thinking. He said with a smile, 'He's just my driver. As I said my car with me and the driver will only take two, so if one of you wouldn't mind going with Arthit in his pick-up. It's quite comfortable. He's a good driver.'

'Didn't he wrap my father round a tree?' remarked Neville.

'It wasn't his fault.'

'Well, I don't fancy driving with him.'

'Nor do I,' put in Jennifer.

'He was responsible for my father's death, after all,' added Neville.

'Why can't we fly to Chiang Mai?' asked Jennifer, petulantly.

'I don't mind travelling with Arthit in his truck,' said Barbara.

36

'Are you sure?' said Peter, relieved. 'The pick-up is brand new.'

'Why can't we fly?' reiterated Jennifer.

'Because Mr Cochrane has kindly arranged for us to go by road,' replied the mother. 'We'll be able to see some of the country.'

The car and the pick-up soon appeared, the luggage was loaded into Arthit's truck and they set off: Barbara with her husband's lover, her children with Peter Cochrane. It was agreed that they should break the four-hundred-mile journey at Kamphaeng Phet and spend the night at a Western-style hotel there, which Peter had assured them 'was perfectly all right'.

24

Toshi turned up at Sylvia's flat as she had hoped. She wasn't absolutely sure that he would come until she heard the chiming doorbell sound at exactly six-thirty – she had not given him back the key which he had left on the hall step after their altercation before Christmas. The Japanese she had discovered, and her discovery had been confirmed by Matthew, were so literal-minded that Toshi might easily have prepared drafts for sixty thousand and thirty thousand yen. The bell dispelled her fears that he had misunderstood. As soon as she opened the door, Toshi flung himself into her arms. There was no one else in the world, Sylvia reflected, who would give her such a manifest sign of affection. They spent a happy night together.

Although she had been dismissed, she was amazed to find that the professors in the Literature Department were so cordial, far more so than they had been previously; even Professor Suzuki, who she knew was mainly responsible for the curtailment of her contract, went out of his way to be pleasant. He revived his visits to her room in the university and as before plied her with questions about Wilde's plays:

'What does it mean, Mrs Field, when Cecily says "When I

see a spade I call it a spade", and Gwendolen answers that she is glad that she has never seen a spade? How can it be that Gwendolen has never seen a spade?'

'Are they sugaring the pill?' Sylvia asked Matthew, one morning when she visited him in his room in the university.

'Yes.'

'Why should they trouble to do so now I'm leaving?'

'They don't like there to be any discord. *Wa*, harmony, is a vital Japanese precept; Confucian, really. They'll give you a goodbye party and the whole thing will end in smiles.'

'It sounds very hypocritical.'

'It is.' After a pause, he asked, 'You'll be taking up the editing job then?'

'Yes, definitely, yes. Toshi came round a few nights ago – we had a screamingly funny conversation on the phone first, I'll tell you about it. Well, Toshi came round. He was sweet. I think I've persuaded him to live with me.'

'Do you really want him to?'

'Yes, I do. It may not work. I feel lonely at night.'

'You live so near the bank. His colleagues may find out.'

'He'll have to cope with that. There's no one in England like Toshi. There was a Japanese, actually, living in the same block of flats as my mother with an old woman—'

Matthew raised his eyebrows.

'She's in her late seventies like my mother. Anyway, I met him and he made me think of Japan, of Toshi, and so I returned, though I was in half a mind not to.'

'I think I shall resign,' said Matthew, who wanted to leave the subject of Sylvia and Toshi and talk about himself and Jun.

'But you have tenure.'

'I know they can't sack me, unless I do something frightful, but when Jun marries – the wedding is fixed for April – I shan't feel like staying on.' He swallowed and his eyes watered. 'Jun has become so much a part of my life.' Matthew and Sylvia were on intimate terms, often seeking advice and sympathy from each other. Sylvia had a certain amount of affection for Jun; although she was prepared to accept gay relationships, being one of those women who are drawn to gays because they find their company agreeable, in her heart of hearts she had reservations about them; she would have been happier if her son, Mark were not living with Colin Sibley, the actor.

'Perhaps you could find a replacement,' suggested Sylvia.

'How can you replace the irreplaceable?' moaned Matthew in the resonant voice of an actor of the old school playing Lear. Somewhat unkindly, he added, 'You've never been in love.'

'I had a husband whom I loved until he ditched me. And there's been Toshi—'

'And the greengrocer?'

Sylvia winced. 'I should never have told you about him. He was no more than a lust figure. Anyway, I've given him up and I think he's given me up; anyway, it's over. And Toshi says he's given up the doctor's wife.'

Matthew laughed. 'A deal has been struck then.'

'You can call it that. We'll see how it works. I'm looking forward to my new job at the publisher's.'

'When does it begin?'

'On the first of April.'

'A propitious day,' said Matthew, seriously.

'I've not heard Fools Day called that before,' said Sylvia, laughing. 'I think I shall find the work more interesting than teaching.'

'Couldn't be less. Between you and me I get fed up with my repetitious performances in the classroom. I tell myself as I've told other foreign teachers here: think of the money and the holidays when you feel frustrated.'

'My salary will be less at the publisher's and I shall have to pay the rent for my flat which up till now the university has been paying.'

'I sometimes feel like walking out of classes because of the lack of response.'

'I hope I shall be able to manage. I don't want to draw on the rent from my London flat or the pittance my ex-husband pays me.'

After a silence, Matthew said, 'Will you come to Jun's wedding? It's to be at Chinzanso, that expensive Japanese restaurant and marriage place where they have several weddings going on at the same time. I shall have to. It's in a beautiful garden setting.'

'I'll come if he'd really like me to.'

'He would. I know he would. He's fond of you.' Matthew sighed. 'What one needs is to be wanted by someone. The main ingredient of happiness is to be wanted.'

'Not, though, by the police,' was Sylvia's riposte to Matthew's sententious utterance.

There came a knock on the door. 'That'll be Mr Kudo for his tutorial,' said Matthew. 'Come in!' he sang out in a professorial tone. The door opened and a young, tall, not unhandsome Japanese student entered the room.

Sylvia rose.

'You know Mrs Field, Kudo-san?' said Matthew.

Kudo bowed; Sylvia smiled and nodded, picked up her handbag and a small hold-all from the table. 'I'm off for a swim.'

'*Gambatté*,' said Matthew.

'What does that mean?' asked Sylvia.

'You don't know what *gambatté* means? The Japanese say it to one another all the time. Don't they, Kudo-san?'

'I'm sorry. I did not hear what you say.'

'*Gambatté*,' said Matthew. 'I said *gambatté* to Mrs Field as she's going swimming.'

'What does it mean?' asked Sylvia, impatiently.

'Tell her, Mr Kudo.'

'Tell her?'

'Tell Mrs Field what *gambatté* means.'

'It means "endure,", er, "endure with fortitude".'

'Good, Kudo-san. It's rather like saying, "Courage", perhaps more like "*courage*" in French, which seems to have more significance than the word does in English. A Japanese friend of mine came back from a trip to England and said he was impressed by the signs he saw everywhere saying, "Take Courage". He didn't realise it was a beer. He thought it was an exhortation by the government.' Matthew laughed and so did Sylvia. Kudo remained solemn.

'What are you studying, Mr Kudo?' asked Sylvia, sweetly.

'Faulkner. The Snopes Trilogy.'

'Well, *gambatté* to you, then.' Sylvia left the room.

25

Leonard and Wilson were reclining on the floor of "My Cup" propped up by cushions. The importunate boys had been fended off; after accepting beers or soft drinks they had ceased their fondling of the two old men, sensing that they were not desired, and had gone off to pet and to pester other foreign prey. 'So none of these are your "cup", Wilson?'

'No, too young, too persistent, too much "on".'

'What do you expect in a place like this. Genteel manners?'

'I'd like them to be a bit older and less brash. To change the subject slightly, have you come to any decision about Trevor?'

'No.'

'You ought to do something for the poor lad.'

'Why? You think I treated him unfairly? He ran out on me. I didn't turn him out.'

'You were unfaithful to him with Yuichi.'

'I explained to him that my dalliance with Yuichi counted for nothing, or for very little anyway. What do you think I ought to do for Trevor, buy him a flat?'

'Yes.'

'Flats cost so much.'

'It needn't be in the West End.'

The platform at the end of the room suddenly lit up and a young man in a G-string came on and started to perform a go-go dance, thrusting his pelvis, his hips, turning and rotating his buttocks.

'Look!' said Leonard.

'I must say,' remarked Wilson, 'he has a splendid physique.'

'Body builder.'

'He appears to be very serious about his lascivious dance,' added Wilson.

'He thinks he's a great artist,' returned Leonard, 'performing great art.'

The young man was succeeded by several more of the bar boys who repeated the provocative gyrations which were a sort of sensual version of running on the spot.

After six boys had gone through their naughty paces the lights went out. There was a fanfare and an announcement came through the loudspeakers: 'We now have "ruv" show.'

'Did my ears hear right?' asked Wilson.

'Yes. He means "fuck show", really.'

'Good heavens!' said Wilson, sitting up.

The lights on the stage came on. Two boys in G-strings brought in a low coffee table and then jogged out. A naked boy with a hand over his genitals appeared, danced around for a few moments, then noticing the table, lay on it and pretended to go to sleep. The body builder entered and seeing the recumbent boy, seized his legs and pulled them up into the air.

'The strung-chicken position,' said Leonard. 'Tried it?'

Indignant, Wilson answered firmly, 'No!'

The boy began to waggle his legs. The body builder slipped off his G-string and began to stimulate his prick with one hand and with the other steadied the legs and pushed them wider apart, and then he seemed to enter his partner, lying on top of him and pumping his buttocks. Both began to groan in rapture. All at once the body builder emitted a shout and gave his partner a brief hug. The couple then disentangled themselves, stood up, faced the audience, and, their hands screening their genitals, smiled like acrobats who have just completed a clever turn.

'Simulated,' said Leonard.

26

Trevor's ears might have been burning when Leonard and Wilson were discussing him in "My Cup", and the old men's too. Veronica had invited Trevor to dinner in her Kensington flat since she knew he was lonely, and she felt sorry for him; also, Veronica was curious about his relationship with Leonard and his quarrel with Yuichi. Over a meal she had given Wilson and Trevor when the Lane family had been in Chiang Mai for Henry's funeral, Trevor had dropped innuendoes concerning himself, Leonard and Yuichi and about Barbara and Yuichi. Now while she had Trevor alone to dinner during another absence of the Lane family in Chiang Mai she started, halfway through the meal, to draw the young man out. Trevor was no match for feminine guile; after a few whiskies and half a bottle of claret he was easily drawn out by Veronica.

'Is Yuichi really gay, d'you think?' she asked.

'He's "bi". I know he had sex with Leonard. Leonard admitted it, and he lived with Jennifer, and he had it off with Barbara. He told me that when we were fightin' on the floor at Grasslands, the Lanes' place. You were there, anyway.'

'I heard nothing. We were all asleep.'

'I kicked him and called him a Japanese bastard and he got me in this judo 'old. You've 'eard the story—'

'Yes, but not from you. Go on.'

'Jennifer put her head round the door and spied on us. She thought we were having sex and then she, mad at Yuichi, drove off to London in the middle of the night. That's about it.'

'Tell me about what Yuichi said about himself and Barbara.'

'Can't. Nothing to tell. He just said 'e 'ad 'er.'

'He may have been romancing,' suggested Veronica.

Trevor shrugged. 'I think 'e 'as 'is eye on the main chance. I think 'e 'as sex in exchange for 'elp'; – when agitated Trevor was inclined to forget the aspirates in the language – 'Leonard 'elped 'im, Jennifer 'ad 'im to live with 'er, and now 'e's spongin' off that old aunt in Hove.'

'You don't suppose he's sleeping with her, do you?'

'Dunno. Do women over seventy want sex? Men of that age do, I know.' Trevor nodded to conform his statement.

'I wonder what will happen when Barbara comes back from Thailand. Will she be jealous of her aunt?'

Trevor laughed. 'Maybe. The Lanes are a kinky lot, aren't they?'

Veronica frowned and poured some more wine into Trevor's glass.

27

'I should like to meet your family,' said Barbara to Arthit as they were driving away from the airport.'

'If you li' I take you see them now.'

'We'd have to go into Bangkok, wouldn't we?'

'Yes.'

'We'd be very late at that place where we're supposed to meet the others.'

'*My pen rai.* Never mi'.'

'They'll be worried. *My pen . . . My pen* what?'

'*My pen rai.*'

'OK let's go and see your family. Never mind.'

Arthit drove towards the capital joining the lines of trucks, cars and buses and motorbikes going in the same direction. The traffic flowed slowly but smoothly until they got into the city where it became clogged up, with long waits at lights.

'You li' radio?' asked Arthit. 'I have cassette.'

'No, thanks.'

'Henry no like radio.'

'Oh?'

During a long wait by a red light clusters of motorbikes threaded their way to the front, nonchalantly squeezing by the cars, seemingly oblivious of the danger. That was the Thai devil-may-care way, Barbara supposed. It took them a good hour and a half to reach the *soi* where Arthit lived with his family; it was an ugly depressing lane consisting of three-storey terrace-houses with entrances as wide as shopfronts. A number of hand carts, bikes, *tuk-tuks* and trucks cluttered the treeless street. Arthit stopped his pick-up outside one of the houses whose wide doors were open behind a concertina grill. He got out and shouted and then helped Barbara to descend. Soon from the back appeared a Chinese-looking woman dressed in jeans and a while sleeveless blouse. She pulled open the grill and let Barbara and Arthit into the long garage-like room, which could easily have accommodated the pick-up; perhaps it did at night. There were no windows. The light came from the door and a long fluorescent strip in the high ceiling. In the room was a table covered by a plastic cloth, round which were four upright chairs; a large television set stood on a wooden crate, and against the wall was an old car seat above which was a calendar depicting a bikini-clad girl embracing a motor tyre.

'This my wife,' muttered Arthit, after speaking in Thai to the woman who had opened the grill.

'How do you do?' said Barbara, holding out her hand towards the woman's *wai* and inclined head. The woman was petite, pale, and she wore no make-up; she looked older than Arthit, who, Barbara knew, was thirty.

Arthit spoke again to his wife, who turned towards the back of the room and shouted something. Barbara was invited to sit at the table.

'You li' *nam manao*? Water with fresh lime.'

'That would be nice.' It was hot in the room, for Barbara at least. She dabbed her forehead with a folded handkerchief.

Why, she wondered, did Thais never seem to be hot. Arthit switched on a standard rotating fan that stood near the table. 'That's better,' said Barbara.

Presently a young Thai girl entered the room with two children. Arthit introduced his offspring to Barbara. 'This my son,' he said, proudly indicating the older of the two. 'And this my daughter.'

'What are their names?' asked Barbara.

'My son is Preecha.'

'Preacher?'

'Yes, Preecha. My daughter is Suporn.'

'Su-*porn*? What a fun – er pretty name.'

Both children were well dressed: Suporn in a clean frock, Preecha in trousers and a sort of smock. Neither wore shoes. Arthit spoke peremptorily to the girl who had brought in the children, now gathered round their parents: Preecha gained his father's knees, Suporn her mother's lap.

'Who is she?' asked Barbara, when the girl had disappeared to a room at the back of the house.

'She the maid,' explained Arthit.

'You have a maid?' Barbara was surprised. Had Henry paid for the maid as well as helping towards the mortgage and other expenses? To have a servant in such a humble dwelling was like nineteenth-century England when only the poorest of the poor were without some sort of domestic help. Barbara wondered how the fifty thousand pounds left to Arthit by Henry would be spent; looking again at the wife, she conjectured that she was less docile than she appeared and that she would probably have a considerable say in how the money would be used. The maid returned with glasses of fresh lime, ice and water for the grown-ups. 'Delicious,' said Barbara. 'Most refreshing.' Arthit let his son sip from his glass.

After a few silent minutes Arthit suggested that it was time for him and Barbara to recommence their journey.

28

'Two hearts,' declared Lady Hinton.

'Two?' exclaimed Winifred, who was playing bridge in Gertrude's flat. Sir Geoffrey Hinton and Colonel Loxley were not invited. On these occasions they played bridge at the Hove Club, a men's four. The female quartette consisted of Lady Hinton, Mrs Loxley, Winifred and Gertrude, the hostess.

'That's very bold of you, partner,' remarked Winifred. She chested her cards and said, 'I've never shown you the portrait Yuichi's painting of me. You must have a look at it.'

'Not now,' said Lady Hinton. 'We can't go up to your flat now to view pictures. We're playing bridge. Two hearts.'

'Two?'

'Yes, two.'

'No bid,' declared Mrs Loxley, who was on Lady Hinton's left.

'I didn't mean now,' said Winifred. 'I meant we might go up to my flat to have a look at it when we stop for tea or when we've finished.'

'If we ever begin,' sighed Lady Hinton.

'I much look forward to seeing it,' said Gertrude.

'Have you heard from Sylvia recently?' asked Winifred, who was still chesting her cards.

'She never writes. She phones me sometimes but never writes.' Gertrude looked at Winifred. 'It was partly due to Yuichi that she went back.'

'Oh? You never told me that when I was lunching with you the other day.'

'Two hearts.'

'No bid.'

'Well, he met Sylvia and they went for a walk along the sea front on a very blustery afternoon, and Sylvia said that meeting him made her decide to go back to Japan; after talking to him she felt homesick for Tokyo.'

'I know all about that,' said Winifred, 'You know what your daughter told Yuichi, don't you?'

'No, what?'

'She has a Japanese lover in Tokyo. That's why she went back.'

'She never told me,' complained Gertrude.

'Perhaps we'd better have a re-deal,' put in Lady Hinton.

'Oh no,' objected Winifred. 'You said two something.'

'Hearts,' Lady Hinton reminded her partner crossly.

'And I said "no bid",' said Mrs Loxley.

'What did I say?'

'You haven't said anything yet, not about your hand at least,' remarked Molly Hinton, pointedly.

'Oh, haven't I? What shall I call then?' She unchested her cards and began to appraise them.

Gertrude leant towards Winifred and lowered her voice. 'I didn't mention this the other day, but do you know what Yuichi told Sylvia?'

'No, what?' Winifred regarded Gertrude suspiciously.

'He said that as well as being Jennifer's lover he had slept with Jennifer's mother.'

Calmly, Winifred answered, 'He told me that too,' She glanced at her cards. 'He's quite a one, my Yuichi,' she added, smugly.

'Two hearts,' interrupted Lady Hinton, almost shouting.

'No bid,' repeated Mrs Loxley.

Winifred frowned over her hand. 'Now what shall I say?'

'He seems quite a Don Juan,' said Gertrude, again addressing Winifred in not much more than a whisper.

'I'm surprised that Yuichi should have told Sylvia, a comparative stranger, about his amorous antics.'

'Two *hearts*,' called Molly Hinton, 'for the umpteenth time. And your opponent has said "No bid".'

Winifred began to estimate her hand. 'I must say something.'

'Please say something, Winifred, but about your hand,' said Molly, 'no more please about your Japanese protégé, fascinating though he sounds.

'And there was that millionaire,' said Gertrude in *sotto voce.*
'You're not suggesting?'
'No, just wondering.'
'*Please*, Winifred,' pleaded Molly in a tone of desperation.
Winifred glanced at her cards. 'Four spades.'
'Are you sure, partner?' asked her ladyship.
'Four spades,' repeated Winifred, defiantly. 'You did say spades, didn't you Molly?'
'No, I said hearts.'
'No bid,' said Gertrude.
'Then perhaps you can go five hearts,' Winifred suggested to Molly.
'I can't possibly.'
'It's me to play, then,' said Winifred, smiling.

29

The telephone rang in Leonard's bedroom in the Golden Plaza Hotel in Chiang Mai. 'Yes?' he answered, irritably. He always treated his callers as if they were intruding upon an important task on which he was engaged – in this case reading a copy of the *Herald Tribune.*
'This is Jennifer.'
'Ah, yes.'
'We've returned.'
'We?'
'My mother, my brother and me.'
'Oh yes, you said you might be coming back for the blessing of your father's gravestone or something.'
'The ceremony is tomorrow. Peter Cochrane, the local manager of Daddy's company, is with us, so is Arthit, the driver. We're staying at the hotel near the Night Market, where you stay. Why did you move?'
'For a change. Wilson is here.'
'I knew he was coming, of course. I'd love to see him.'

'I expect you will.'

'Leonard, can you do something for me?'

'What?' Leonard was not a good angel of mercy, unless there was something in the act of benevolence for him. He managed to put into his monosyllabic interrogative a considerable amount of unwillingness and indifference.

'Please can you help me find Somsak.'

'Somsak?' Leonard knew perfectly well whom Jennifer meant; it amused him to feign ignorance.

'Somsak. You know Somsak. We met him at that disco. I told you about him when you took me round the museum.'

'I remember vaguely. What do you want me to do?'

'Help me find him.' Jennifer sounded distraught.

'I don't know where he lives,' objected Leonard.

'I have his school address. Would you come there with me?'

A pause.

'Leonard, are you still there?' Jennifer asked anxiously.

'Yes, I am. I was pondering over your request. I think Wilson would be a more effective cicerone than I, and you know him far better than you know me. Why don't you ring him? He's staying in this hotel, in the next room, in fact.'

'OK, I will. Thanks.'

'Goodbye.'

30

The journey in Peter Cochrane's car and in Arthit's pick-up had passed off without any untoward incident. Jennifer, Neville and Peter had been anxious when Barbara and Arthit arrived two hours later than they had at the hotel in Kamphaeng Phet, a Western-style establishment on the Ping river.

'Oh, Mummy, we were so worried,' Jennifer wailed. 'What happened? And all our luggage was in the truck.'

'Arthit took me to see his family in Bangkok.'

'We thought you might have had an accident,' said Neville, glaring at Arthit.

Barbara's object in travelling in Arthit's pick-up was to try and discover more about the Thai's relationship with her husband. What had he seen in this rather ordinary looking man with the rough voice? Arthit had told her that Henry had been fond of his children. 'And what about your wife?'

'He no like her.' Arthit laughed raucously.

While he drove the pick-up slowly out of Bangkok, past the airport and on to Ayuttaya and the north, Barbara mused about her husband's affair with Arthit. Had Henry been homosexual all along, since before their marriage? Or had he not known his true tastes before meeting Arthit? And why had Henry been bowled over by this man? To be infatuated by a slim, lithe, pretty, seductive, sexy Thai boy or girl would be understandable. There seemed to be little differentiation between the sexes among the Thais, at least when they were young; it was as if they retained the androgyny of childhood until their late teens, although the male appendage and the female breasts protruded so little as to be barely noticeable. Why fall for this unprepossessing Thai? He wasn't ugly exactly, but plain, except when he smiled, then his face became pleasing. The only answer Barbara could find was that sexual attraction was unfathomable. She didn't know much about sex. With Henry it had never been satisfactory; she had never enjoyed it. After their second child, Jennifer, had been born, their sexual activity had ceased, and for the last few years they had slept in different rooms. Barbara had given up prurient thoughts until recently, when desire had been awakened by Yuichi, who at that time was her daughter's lover. It had only happened once on a wintry afternoon in Jennifer's London flat when Jennifer had been at work. Barbara, at fifty-two, had not experienced anything so exciting in her life. Just before she left for Thailand with her son and daughter for the blessing of Henry's stone, she had gone down to Hove to say goodbye to Aunt Winifred. After lunch, when the old lady had retired to rest, Yuichi, who was then living with Winifred, had made a provocative gesture at the door as she was leaving the flat. He had taken off his pullover, undone his shirt buttons to his navel, half unzipped his trousers and put his fingers on his crotch. 'You no like?' he had said. 'No,' Barbara had replied. She hurried home to Grasslands. Now, sitting beside her deceased husband's lover, who was concentrating on the task of driving, Yuichi came to her mind again: Yuichi on that afternoon in Jennifer's flat; Yuichi making that lustful pose at the door of Winifred's apartment in Hove. Why did she think of him? Because those few moments of making love with him on her daughter's sofa had been sheer ecstasy. She wished now that she had not resisted his act of incitement.

'Arthit?'

'Yes, Mrs Rane?'

'What will you do with the money Henry left you?'

'I no yet decide. My wife she want open restaurant. I no want. I mus' give my father some money. He is very poor and he owe money.'

'Of course you must. Henry left the money to you. You must do as you please with it.' Barbara thought of what was to her Arthit's awful house: the garage-like doors with the concertina shutters, the car seat, the TV set on a packing case, the harsh strip light. She thought of the simplicity of his home, and the discomfort; she did not regret the fifty thousand pounds her husband had left him. Arthit seemed a good honest man, unsophisticated and undereducated, nevertheless reliable and trustworthy. Given Henry's latent development as a homosexual, he might well have taken up with some venal, calculating, exploiting boy from a bar. That he hadn't was either due to his cautiousness, his discernment, or to his luck. A bit of each, perhaps.

31

It was after ten in the morning. Leonard, no early riser, had just finished his breakfast, which was brought to him in his room.

He hated joining the tourists in the Coffee Shop, where the meal was laid out buffet style, and one had to queue for orange juice, cereal or papaya and wait by the pop-up toaster for one's toast, which was sometimes grabbed by a greedy guest. Many of the tourists behaved as if they had been deprived of food for days and were afraid that the provisions would all be eaten up before they had helped themselves. It was extraordinary how they piled their plates with croissants, brioches and toast. Most of them came from Western Europe. Where had they been brought up?

Leonard sat back in his armchair and took up *Sense and Sensibility*, borrowed from Wilson, who had lent it to him reluctantly. 'I haven't finished it,' Wilson complained.

'You won't want it in the graveyard, will you? You'll be praying there, won't you? And I presume you've read it before. So you know what happens.'

Wilson left to meet the Lanes at their hotel, and to accompany them to the British cemetery for the blessing of the gravestone. Peter Cochrane had made the arrangements.

Wilson heaved himself out of the *tuk-tuk* he had hired and paid the driver sixty *baht*. He knew it was too much, but bargaining with the rapacious *tuk-tuk* men was tedious and undignified. Immediately he stepped into the hotel lobby, Jennifer ran up to him.

'Oh, Wilson, it's sweet of you to come!'

'I was fond of your father, you know.'

'Mummy will be down soon. Neville and Peter Cochrane are here, and so is Arthit, Daddy's er, Daddy's friend.'

Wilson shook hands with the members of the party, eyeing Arthit, whom he had not met before. Being of the same persuasion as Henry, he saw the Thai in a different light from the others. Barbara Lane appeared. She had made up her face carefully, but her eyes looked tired. She was wearing a simple white dress whose sleeves came down to just below her elbows, and over her head she wore a black lace kerchief, a sort of mantilla.

Peter, Neville and Wilson were, in spite of the air-conditioning in the lobby, looking hot in their dark summer suits, but Arthit in a short-sleeved white shirt with black tie seemed quite cool.

'Very good of you to come, Wilson,' said Barbara. 'I'm not late, am I?' she asked, turning to Peter Cochrane.

'No, Mrs Lane, but we'd better get going. Arthit can take one in his pick-up and I three. My driver is not coming.'

'I'll go in the pick-up,' volunteered Wilson, who, self-effacing, liked to be helpful, and also he wanted a chance to talk to Arthit.

As he and the Thai driver set off for the cemetery, Wilson regarded Henry's lover. He realised what Henry had seen in him. Arthit was not good-looking, but his smile was charming and his manner pleasant; his masculinity was tempered by a delicate gentleness, manifested by the way he helped Wilson into the pick-up.

'I knew Henry well,' said Wilson as the truck edged its way through a street cluttered on either side with stalls selling food, fruit, clothes and plastic kitchen utensils.

'He my good friend,' stated Arthit.

'I know.'

'He tell you about me?'

'Yes.'

'What he say?'

'That you were his good friend.' Wilson did not mention any of the details of Arthit's abilities which Henry had imparted to him.

32

Leonard put down his book, shut his eyes and thought of Yuichi. Why was it that the young Japanese kept invading his mind, even when reading Jane Austen? He had been so exciting, more so than anyone Leonard could recall. Trevor in comparison was a lump of cold meat. The English were hopeless lovers. There was something about Yuichi that was different. He made love with imagination, knowing what would arouse a sixty-year-old. Leonard had lusted after Jim, the Thai barman in one of the bars in the Night Market in Chiang Mai, but since Jim had parried his advances, stood him up several times, and flirted with Barbara at a party Leonard had given, Leonard had decided to cease his attempt to seduce him. He had wasted so much time thinking about Jim, and had drunk too many Thai whiskies at his bar. And now with *Sense and Sensibility* on his lap, Yuichi entered his thoughts, which became increasingly concupiscent. He put a hand on his crotch. There was a knock. 'Damn!' Leonard went to the door. 'Later. *Yung mai set*,' he said to the maid, who wanted to do his room. He closed the door and began his matutinal ablutions.

33

After the conversation with Gertrude about Yuichi and Sylvia that had held up the bidding on that bridge afternoon and greatly annoyed Molly Hinton, Winifred decided she would speak to Yuichi about the indiscreet revelations he had made to Sylvia. She waited a few days and one evening while they were eating spaghetti carbonara (a dish Yuichi did well) in the kitchen, Winifred, after the Japanese had refilled her wine glass and his, said, 'Yuichi, why did you tell Sylvia about your amorous exploits?'

'Uh?' Yuichi didn't really like to talk during the serious business of eating. He flicked his eyes up at Winifred and then looked down at his plate on which half the huge helping he had given himself remained. With his spoon and fork he deftly rolled some spaghetti into a wad which he put into his mouth; bit off the dangling ends and let them drop on to his plate; his table manners had been better at Grasslands, Winifred remarked to herself.

The old lady sighed. 'Yuichi, you told Sylvia Field, Gertrude's daughter, that you went to bed with Jennifer and with Barbara, her mother.'

'*So des.*'

'What?'

'It is true.'

'Why did you tell Sylvia?'

'It bad to tell her?'

'Yes, because you did not know her well.'

'I tell you,' said Yuichi filling his mouth again with spaghetti and ham.

'Yes, but that is different.'

'How different?'

'Because, because,' began Winifred, flustered. 'Because you are living with me. We are close. I am not a stranger. Why did you tell her?'

'We talk about Tokyo. She tell me she have lover in Tokyo. I tell her I have lover in Rondon, but I have fight with her and I have her mother.'

'Just an exchange of information, I see. It's not good to divulge, to tell about intimate experiences to someone you don't know well.'

'*Ah so, deska?*'

'What does that mean?' she demanded crossly.

'It mean same as English – er, let me see – er "is that so" you say, right?'

'Well, never mind.' Winifred knew she would get no further with her inquiry, which she now wished she hadn't started, but she did ask him about Leonard.

'He very kind to me,' replied Yuichi.

'Why?'

'He like me. Why you ask me like this, like policeman. You angry with me?'

'No, no Yuichi.'

'If you angry with me, I go. You like I go?' He looked at her, eyes black as ebony, dull, yet full of a fury that was alarming.

'No, no, please don't. Please stay. I need you.'

'OK, I stay, but I say what I like to anyone.'

34

Under the great trees in the cemetery stood the mourners waiting for the Thai Presbyterian minister, who was late. There being no Anglican church in Chiang Mai, the Lanes had to make do with a minister from the Presbyterian Mission.

On the marble slab set into the laterite plinth was engraved:

> In Memory of
> Henry Lupert Lane
> (1937–1994)
> This stone was placed
> by his fond family:
> his wife, Barbara,
> his son, Neville, his daughter, Jennifer.
> RIP
> He loved Thailand

The group gathered by the gravestone. Barbara smiled. 'At least the engraver got "Lane" right. I rather like "Lupert".'

'It must be changed,' said Neville. 'I suppose it can be. Can it, Peter?'

'I'll see to it.'

'I don't mind the mistake,' said Barbara. 'It makes it charmingly Thai somehow. Henry would have been amused. Let's keep it as it is.'

'Oh, Mummy, I agree,' concurred Jennifer.

The Presbyterian minister arrived in a *tuk-tuk*. A slim man, dark-skinned and wearing glasses, he was dressed in a flimsy black gown made of nylon with two white ministerial bands at his neck. Holding a prayer book in his right hand, he greeted the party with a *wai*, and then there was a pause during which the mourners bowed their heads and waited. The minister approached Peter Cochrane and whispered a few words.

'He wants to know what you'd like him to do.' said Peter out of the corner of his mouth to Barbara.

'Doesn't he know? Didn't you tell him? We'd like him to say a prayer for Henry and then bless the tomb.'

The minister muttered what sounded like the Lord's Prayer and then said quietly in a heavy Thai accent, 'We come here from far and near, to commemorlate our brother Henly at his final place of rest, and we bress this memorial in the name of the Lord.' The minister raised his right hand, and after a minute's silence he turned from the gravestone and solemnly shook hands with the mourners except Arthit, to whom he gave a *wai*.

'Thank you,' said Barbara.

'Is that all?' complained Neville. 'We've come all this way for that?'

'What did you expect? Mozart's Requiem with orchestra, choir and soloists?' returned Jennifer.

'I feel better now I've seen the stone and had it blessed. But we should have brought flowers.' said Barbara.

While Peter was talking to the minister and paying him for his services, Barbara and Neville got into his car. 'Jennifer!' cried Barbara. 'Aren't you coming?'

'I'm going with Wilson and Arthit. See you later at the hotel.'

35

'Arthit,' said Jennifer in a commanding tone after she and Wilson had squeezed into the cabin of the pick-up, 'please drive us to this school.' She handed the Thai a well-worn piece of paper on which was written the address of the school where Somsak Chutanam was the art master.

'I don't think you need me, do you?' said Wilson. "Perhaps you could drop me off at the Golden Plaza, if you're going that way.'

'Oh no, Wilson. Please come. I need moral support.'

'You have Arthit.'

'He lacks authority. You look just what's needed: important, sagacious. They respect the old. And you did say you'd help me find Somsak on the phone.'

Wilson laughed. 'I didn't know I looked sagacious. All right. But I must be back at the hotel for lunch. Leonard will be cross if I'm not.'

They skirted the left bank of the River Ping, crossed Nawarat Bridge and entered Tapae Road, the main drag, a one-way street bustling with disorderly traffic. At Tapae Gate, a recent reconstruction, they had to follow the moat until they crossed a bridge into the old city; along the moat they went, past an ancient piece of fortified wall, and then turned west with the moat still on their right. They passed the remains of a gate in the ramparts.

'Chang Puak Gate, White Elephant Gate, the northern gate of the old city,' explained Wilson.

'White Elephant Gate,' repeated Jennifer awesomely. 'What a wonderful name! I adore this place.'

Soon they were out of the old city and going up Huey Kaew Road. At a crossing by the Golden Plaza they were held up by traffic lights. The fumes from the exhausts of the vehicles around them were asphyxiating. Arthit switched on the air conditioning and shut the windows.

'Good,' said Wilson.

'I don't mind a whiff of carbon dioxide,' said Jennifer. To her everything in Chiang Mai was marvellous and she was going to see Somsak, whom she loved.

'Monoxide,' corrected Wilson.

They passed several apartment blocks and hotels, overpowering, grim and unimaginative, the gates of Chiang Mai University and an arboretum.

'The school is somewhere on the right, as far as I can remember. I only saw it in the dark, though,' said Jennifer.

Arthit drew into the side of the road, jumped out of the pick-up and crossed the road, spoke to someone on the pavement and skipped back across the busy thoroughfare.

'It is there.' He pointed across the road.

'I knew it was,' said Jennifer.

They entered a bowery drive of coconut palms, banana trees and dark-leafed shrubs ('Mango trees,' Wilson informed Jennifer, who wasn't interested) and came to a rectangular, functional building with an open space in front of it dominated by a white flagpole from which drooped the Thai flag on this windless, cloudless, sunny morning. There was no one about, but the buzz of teaching was audible. A few cars, pick-ups and a host of motor-scooters were parked nearby. The visitors alighted from their vehicle. Jennifer said, 'Arthit, please go and ask where Mr Somsak Chutanam is.'

Obediently, the driver went into the building. After a few minutes he reappeared with a man in a khaki shirt and trousers with a casual polyester jacket slung over his shoulders. He directed Arthit with a number of gestures and soon the trio was back in the pick-up passing other featureless, functional buildings. They came to the end of the campus, turned through a gap between two palms and stopped outside a shack with a corrugated-iron roof.

'This is it,' said Jennifer. She stretched across Wilson and sounded Arthit's horn. There were similar shacks among the trees.

'Government housing?' Wilson inquired.

A mongrel rushed out of the hut barking.

Jennifer was out of the pick-up before Arthit had time to run round and open the door, but in time to assist Wilson to alight. 'Hello,' Jennifer said to the dog, dangling a hand, which was licked.

'You should be careful of dogs here,' warned Wilson.

'Oh, phooey!' said the girl. Presently, Somsak emerged. He

was dressed in jeans, a blue shirt and sandals and he was holding a cat in his arms. Jennifer hurried towards him. 'Somsak!' she cried, stretching out her arms, her black handbag swaying on her left wrist. The young Thai teacher lowered the cat gently to the ground and fended off Jennifer's attempt to hug him by grasping her hands.

'Did you get my letter?'

'No.'

'Oh Somsak, I'm so pleased to see you.' She turned to Wilson and Arthit, who were watching the scene of reunion, and introduced them; then looking at Somsak again, she exclaimed excitedly, 'You've let your hair grow. I'm so pleased. I hated that short, spikey style you had before.'

'Please come in my hou',' invited Somsak. They all followed him into the hut; it was no more than that, consisting of one room. He kicked off his sandals as he entered. Arthit took off his shoes and Jennifer copied him, but Wilson remained shod.

'I have no more chair,' said Somsak, indicating the one chair in the room, an upright one, and at the same time giving a disarming smile. His looks matched his charm: large dark eyes and fine raven locks. The fact that unhesitatingly he had invited them into his modest dwelling was, thought Wilson, a plus in his favour.

'What's wrong with the floor?' Jennifer sat on the worn linoleum that partly covered the floor boards, and crossed her legs, oriental style. Arthit sat on the low bed.

'The trouble is,' said Wilson, a heavy man, 'that if I get down there I shall never be able to get up again.' He was sweating. He mopped his face with a handkerchief. 'May I take off my jacket?'

'Of course,' said Jennifer, adding, 'and you take the chair,' as if she were the hostess. Wilson did as he was instructed. Looking round the room Jennifer spotted a drawing on an easel. She jumped up and went over to examine it. 'You're doing abstract, or semi-abstract. Good. The tree is well done. Is it a tree?'

'You li' coffee?' asked Somsak.

'That would be lovely,' said Jennifer.

'I have only two cups. What abou' juice?'

'We'll all have juice,' said Jennifer, resuming her place on the floor.

A chicken clucked its way into the room from the back.

'You have chickens, Somsak?'

'Yes. I have fourteen.'

'Heavens!'

Somsak produced from the refrigerator in a corner a half-empty plastic bottle of Sprite and poured a little of the soft drink into glasses. He explained that he had a class in ten minutes so they all drank up their Sprite quickly and rose. Jennifer arranged for Somsak to go to her hotel that evening, and soon the trio was motoring back towards Chiang Mai.

'Why don't you lunch with Leonard and me at the Golden Plaza,' Wilson suggested to Jennifer.

'I'd love to. Arthit, drop me off at the Golden Plaza.'

'OK. I wait for you?'

'No. I'll go back to the hotel in a *tuk-tuk*.'

As soon as the truck drew up at the hotel entrance, Arthit leapt out and hastened round to open the passenger door. Jennifer shunned the driver's offer of assistance, saying 'See you,' curtly, but Wilson gratefully took Arthit's helping hand, and said, 'Thanks, my boy. Thanks.'

Wilson led Jennifer away from the entrance steps and down a murky passage under the Coffee Shop faintly lit by the fluorescent lights of neighbouring shops displaying shirts, blouses and bolts of Thai silk. At the end of this short tunnel of haberdashery they turned right, mounted some steps and came upon the pool. The blue water was surrounded by blue sunbeds and blue and white parasols; the background was green, purple, red and yellow: the green of the trees, the purple, red and white of the bougainvillaea and the yellow flowers of the cassia trees. In the pool was one bald head, slowly emerging and submerging;

on the sunbeds white Western bodies were outstretched. The eyes of the tourists were either shut or screened by dark glasses, and their faces wore slight frowns as if their thoughts were serious; they gave the impression of being engaged in important work and it seemed they would not lightly brook interruption.

The sole swimmer was Leonard.

'Hello!' shouted Wilson. 'Look who I've brought to see you.'

Leonard turned on his back and waved. 'Can't see without my glasses. Who is it?'

'It's me, Jennifer.'

'Oh, hello,' cried Leonard lukewarmly.

He swam to the steps at the deep end, and holding on to the rails, half out of the water, he called out, 'Wilson, my things are just over there. You'll recognise my Panama. Please bring the hotel bathrobe, my glasses and my hat.' Leonard had no desire to expose his swollen, hirsute body to Jennifer. Wilson obeyed the request and Leonard climbed out of the pool and into the bathrobe held by his tractable friend. Leonard put on his glasses and his Panama. 'Well, how did it go?' he asked Jennifer while trying to tie the waistband of his robe in a bow; the band was too short or Leonard's paunch was too large, so he just made the first twist of a granny knot.

'The ceremony, d'you mean?'

'Let's sit round a table. I prefer straight-backed chairs to the ones you have to loll in. What will you have? You don't want one of these luscious ice-cream concoctions, do you?' He handed a menu with photographs of 'Tropical Temptation', 'Papaya Sunset', 'Lotus Delight', 'Pineapple Prince', and 'Banana of Dreams' to Jennifer, who looked at them and shook her head. 'What about a gin and tonic, then?'

'I'd love one.'

'So would I,' said Wilson.

Leonard signalled to one of the waiters who was standing behind the bar that had a folksy wooden tiled roof half-covered with bougainvillaea. The waiter in a blue shirt and brief shorts had a pleasant face, a beaming smile, a boyish snub nose and sturdy, glabrous legs at which Wilson gazed while Leonard gave the order.

'So the ceremony passed off satisfactorily?' asked Leonard of Jennifer.

'It lasted no more than two minutes. The priest or the minister whatever you call him, a Presbyterian, said a prayer, "bressed" the gravestone, he was a Thai, shook hands with us and that was all.'

'Sounds sensible. Long-drawn out ceremonies are no better than short ones. The point is made and that's it.'

'Afterwards, Arthit, my father's Thai friend, drove us to Somsak's school and he's coming to see me tonight. I'm so excited.'

Leonard grunted.

The barboy arrived with the drinks which he fussily placed on mats on the table. Wilson glanced at his legs, 'Splendid,' he muttered to himself.

Leonard pushed his Panama to the back of his head, put a pair of sunglasses over his spectacles, picked up his tumbler and said, 'Here's luck!' A tripper on a package tour, one might say, thought Wilson, but if one said so Leonard would be very indignant.

36

'We really should have brought flowers,' said Barbara, who was lunching with Neville and Peter Cochrane in their hotel.

'I can get some this afternoon,' replied Peter.

'Tomorrow morning would be better. I'm so tired after the flight from London, that drive. I shall go to bed and stay there until tomorrow.'

'So shall I,' said Neville.

'When are you thinking of returning to the UK?' asked Peter, pointedly.

'In a week or so, perhaps,' answered Barbara. 'I can't face the long flight back yet. I shall have to get over the flight out here before I do.'

'Please let me know in good time so I can book your flight.'

'First class is not likely to be full, is it? It wasn't coming out.'

'No,' admitted Peter.

'I wonder where Jennifer is.'

'Arthit took her to find her so-called Thai lover,' said Neville. 'I told you.'

'What am I to do with my wayward daughter, Peter?'

'Get her home as soon as possible, I should think.'

'She's determined to stay here with her Thai, whom she barely knows. Carnally she knows him, I suppose, judging by today's standards and hers. But is that enough? Hardly. Peter, you know Thailand well, perhaps you could tell my headstrong daughter about the unsuitability of a liaison with a Thai who has no money to speak of. Speak to her of the pitfalls of life here for an inexperienced Western girl.'

'I'll try,' said Peter, half-heartedly.

'I wouldn't call Jennifer inexperienced,' Neville put in.

'She is as far as the East is concerned,' said the mother.

'There was that Jap,' Neville reminded Barbara.

'But he was in London.' The reference to Yuichi made her blush. She quickly changed the subject. Turning to Peter, she asked, 'When is Arthit returning to Bangkok?'

'This afternoon.'

'So soon.'

'He has to get back to the office, and there's his family.'

'Please tell him to come and see me before he goes. I should like to say goodbye to him.'

'Certainly, if he hasn't gone already. And I must go back tomorrow or the day after.'

'Don't bother about booking our flight. The hotel can do that, surely.'

65

37

'What's he like?' asked Leonard.

'I thought you met him when the Lanes were here for the funeral just after Christmas.'

The two old men were still by the pool. Jennifer had left them after rapidly consuming a steak sandwich.

'I did for a moment. It was in a disco bar – Jennifer asked me to take her there. He came up to our table and took her off to dance or to jog about; one can hardly call it dancing. I got a glimpse only. He seemed handsome, very hetero looking, not my type. What did you think, Wilson?'

'I thought he was splendid. Such good manners. He invited us into his humble hut, which had a corrugated iron roof and only a few sticks of furniture: a bed, a chair, a table, not much else. He made no apologies for its inadequacies. He behaved quite naturally. Jennifer gushed. He served us with half a glass each of some dreadful soft drink, but he did it with aplomb, as if it were champagne. I was impressed by his self-assurance. He's certainly someone.'

'H'mm. I'll take you to see Jim tonight.'

'Who's Jim?'

'Certainly someone, as you would say. He runs a bar in the Night Market. Your type. I've never been able to make any headway with him, but you might.'

'I don't see how I could possibly succeed where you've failed.'

'Faint heart . . ., Wilson. He's worth looking at anyway.'

38

It was nine o'clock. Neville came out of the lift and noticed his mother handing in her room key at the desk. He hid behind some potted palms until she had left the hotel. Peter came up to him.

'Your mother's just gone out.'

'I know. I saw her.'

'Have a drink.' They went over to the bar in the open-plan lobby. A piano was accompanying a violin in a selection of tunes by Irving Berlin 'What's yours?'

'Oh, a gin and tonic, please,' Neville looked round the lounge. 'Have you seen Jennifer?'

'She went upstairs with a young Thai.'

'She found him then. Where's Arthit?'

'He went back to Bangkok.'

'I hope he said goodbye to my mother. She wanted to see him before he left.'

'Yes, he did. She saw him just after lunch before she went up to rest.'

'Where did she slink off to? D'you know?'

'Shopping in the Night Market, I expect. It's just up the street. I didn't waylay her. She seemed to be in a hurry.'

Neville downed his drink.

'I think I'll go in search of her. Perhaps it's not good for her to be out on her own.'

'I'll come with you.'

'Please don't bother. I shan't be long. Thanks for the drink.' He didn't want Peter's company. He had ideas of his own and they did not include being with his mother.

39

The pavements of the Night Market were cluttered with stalls selling nothing Barbara wanted: costume jewellery, silverware, lacquerware, socks, T-shirts emblazoned with slogans, shawls, belts, rows of wooden elephants, plastic alarm clocks in psychedelic colours, 'genuine' Swiss watches and all sorts of other trash. There was only a narrow way between the stalls and Barbara had to squeeze past other tourists, many of whom seemed attracted by the wares. She knew how to get to Jim's Bar. She turned left by a shop selling cassettes and CDs out of which boomed the thump of pop din. The passage was dark and the uneven floor boards were not easy to negotiate with her high-heeled shoes. She stumbled along and when she reached the bar no one was there except a young Thai girl, small in stature, wearing a brief miniskirt and a sleeveless blouse. Barbara had a vague notion that she had been introduced to her by Jim as his sister. She climbed on to a bar stool and ordered a Mekong whiskey with soda and a squeeze of lime as Leonard had done when he had brought her to this bar a few weeks ago. The girl understood her order, which was a relief; trying to mime a lime wasn't easy. While the drink was being prepared Barbara gazed at the banknotes from all over the world that decorated the back wall of the dimly lit little bar. There were many she didn't know. When the girl had put the whiskey in front of her on the bar, Barbara asked, 'Where is Jim?'

'He go Lampang.'

'Lampang? Where is that?'

'Not so far. His home Lampang. Maybe he come back tomorrow.'

40

Neville had left his wallet in the safe in his bedroom – he did not want it emptied like last time – and put a small number of *baht* banknotes in his left trouser pocket. 'Fifty pounds ought to be enough for here,' he told himself. He walked up the ill-lit Loi Kroa road, which led to the moat of the old city. He turned right and went along the street on the side of which was the stagnant moat embellished by illuminated fountains and on the other, the side he took, were motorbike shops, business premises and garden cafés with fairy lights. In one of the cafés were girls. 'Where you go?' asked one of them. 'You go with me?' Neville was embarrassed. He wanted sex but he did not wish to sit in a bar buying expensive drinks for a hostess who didn't attract him. He continued on his uncertain way. On the other side of the busy road was an open space backed by a wall in which there was tall, wooden gate – Tapae Gate, in fact. With difficulty – drivers took scant notice of pedestrians – Neville managed to cross over to the open space and here he strolled about. He sat on a stone bench under a tree and watched figures gliding along in the darkness by the wall, near some trees, and by the moat which emerged behind him from under the open space. A man with three poodles, who pranced and barked, circumambulated the space purposefully, no doubt performing a nightly task.

'Hello, where you go?' said a Thai voice of intermediate pitch.

Neville looked round and saw a dark girl standing behind his seat. 'I'm not going anywhere, ' he replied.

The girl came round to his side of the bench and sat by him. She was wearing baggy black trousers and a long multicoloured, silk Chinese jacket with a high collar; dangling from a wrist was a shiny black handbag that clashed with her oriental outfit. Her untidy hair tumbled down to her shoulders; her face was maquillé: red lips, a dab of rouge on each cheek and plucked, pencilled eyebrows. She put a hand tipped with red on Neville's knee. 'You li' me? I li' you.'

Neville cleared his throat. His heart was racing and sweat broke out on his brow. Her little hand moved up his thigh and on to his crotch. His prick was already erect. She grasped it.

'You come with me? We go hotel. No problem. OK?' She squeezed his throbbing penis. 'OK?'

'OK,' Neville croaked. He rose from the bench and they set off together, he towering above her. They went along by the moat, past concrete benches on which people sat, some of them foreign. He strode forward and to keep up with him she took little running steps. She was wearing grubby trainers, Neville noticed; with the handbag, another incongruity, he thought. They waited for a gap in the traffic and then hurried across the road. She took hold of his hand and led him up a dark alley. He stopped. 'How much?' he asked.

'One thou-*sand*.'

'Too much. No.' Neville started to retreat.

'OK, eight hundred.'

'OK.'

She skipped ahead and went into the doorway of a small hotel. Neville followed. Behind a desk in a tiny hall at the foot of a flight of stairs sat a middle-aged Thai man watching television, his eyes not leaving the screen. 'We mus' pay four hun-*dred*,' said the girl. Neville paid and they climbed two flights of steep stairs to a room. She opened the door and quickly went over to the bed and turned on a lamp with a crimson shade and a weak bulb.

'Let's have some more light on the scene,' said Neville. 'Where's the switch?'

'No,' the girl replied firmly. 'I no like.' She went up to him, undid his shirt and then unzipped his trousers, pulling them down to his ankles. He kicked off his shoes and she slid off his socks, pushed him on to the bed, pulled off his trousers, his underpants, his shirt and his vest. She kissed him passionately and started to masturbate him fast. 'No,' objected Neville, brushing aside her eager hand. 'You undress, you take off.' He took hold of her jacket and tugged it. 'Take off,' he commanded.'

'I no li'.'

'I go.' Neville got off the bed and picked up his underpants from the chair where she had thrown his clothes.

'OK.' She took off her Chinese jacket and trousers and stood before him in her slip and brassière.

'No. Take off.' Neville put a finger under her slip. She obeyed and Neville looked but it was too murky to see anything except a thick bush of pubic hair. He put a hand on her breasts. They were flat. He lay on the bed and she placed herself by his side, wriggling and kissing and sucking his cock. She performed fellatio expertly. Neville groaned. She then leapt across the room, took a condom out of her handbag and slipped it over Neville's penis. She straddled him and leant forwards over his body, her head on his chest; she bit his nipple and he came. She was off him in a flash and deftly peeled off the condom. Neville noticed the hand she put over her crotch as she crossed the room to the pile of her clothes on the floor. He jumped off the bed, dashed to the door and turned on the ceiling light, a glaring fluorescent one; in his powerful hands he gripped the little whore's arms and saw what she had been trying to conceal: a penis the size of a walnut. He was furious. He showed his anger by kicking the Chinese garments into the air. The boy was frightened; the foreigner was so much bigger than he. Neville hurled on his clothes, threw a five-hundred *baht* banknote at the cowering lad saying, 'You don't deserve this. I suppose you need it,' and hastened out of the hotel, leaving the boy on his haunches gathering up his pathetic drag.

41

Before Barbara had finished her whiskey, which she sipped as if it were medicine, Leonard and Wilson appeared; the former was cool, the latter warmly welcoming.

'Hello, Barbara! Fancy meeting you in this insalubrious place! Leonard brought me here.' He didn't add that Leonard hoped to see Jim.

'Leonard brought me here too,' said Barbara, 'last time I was in Chiang Mai.'

Wilson sat next to Barbara; Leonard heaved himself on to a stool on Wilson's other side. 'Whisky?' he said to Wilson.

'Please.'

'It'll be that Thai stuff.'

'Never mind.'

While Leonard was ordering two Thai whiskies with soda and lime, Barbara said to Wilson, 'I couldn't sleep. My body clock, whatever you call it, is still keeping English time. This is the only bar I know.' She didn't add that, like Leonard, she had hoped to see the handsome Jim.

'Lampang?' Leonard was saying to the barmaid. 'What's he doing there . . . his home? Oh, I see.' Obviously feeling that out of courtesy he must address Barbara, whom he had not only met but entertained twice on her previous visit, said to her, 'I hear that the ceremony went off satisfactorily.'

'It was very short. The priest, a Thai, didn't quite know what to do. He just greeted us and then blessed the tombstone. By the way, Jim's gone home. Did she tell you?'

'Yes, she did,' answered Leonard, annoyed that Barbara should refer to Jim and that she had inquired about him.

The whiskies Leonard had ordered were placed in front of him and Wilson. Leonard raised his glass. '*Chok dee*,' he said to Wilson.

'*Chok dee*,' repeated his friend. 'What does it mean? I seem to have heard it before, but I've forgotten.'

'It means "cheerio".'

'Easy to say unlike most Thai words.'

'Where is Jennifer?' asked Leonard of Barbara, knowing full well what the answer would be.

'With her Thai friend, the art teacher, I suppose.'

'Have you met him?' asked Leonard.

'Yes. He was at that party you gave just before I left last time. Don't you remember?'

'Of course,' replied Leonard. 'It's strange that both Jennifer's recent boyfriends should be artists, or have artistic pretensions.'

'A peculiar penchant for painters,' put in Wilson, giving a little chuckle.

'I was thinking about Yuichi this morning,' went on Leonard. 'Don't know why. Did you meet him?'

'Yes.' Barbara's face began to colour; fortunately in the dim light of the bar her blushes weren't noticeable. 'A charming young man.' She couldn't add that the Japanese was to her the most exciting person she had ever met. Did Leonard, she wondered, feel the same.

'He's now living in Hove with your aunt, I understand,' said Leonard.

'That's right. How did you know?'

'I told him,' confessed Wilson.

'Ah, did you, now?' remarked Barbara. 'Please don't move, either of you, but I'd better go back to the hotel.'

Both men tumbled off their bar stools.

'We must accompany you,' said Wilson.

'No need, thank you. I know the way. I got here on my own. It's not far.' Barbara started off along the rickety passage.

'Well, well,' exclaimed Leonard, struggling back on to his perch. 'The Lanes are an odd lot. She was after Jim, very much my "cup", and he'd be yours too.'

The barmaid approached and murmured something into Leonard's ear. 'What's that? She didn't pay for her drink? Yes, of course, I'll pay for it.'

Wilson laughed. 'She got a drink out of you, anyhow. We ought to have escorted her back to her hotel.'

'Ought we?'

'It would have been chivalrous.'

Leonard gave his friend a mischievous grin. 'Don't feel chivalrous tonight, and she came here by herself.'

'Leonard, I shall have to be going home soon. That I haven't found the love of my life, as you suggested I might, doesn't bother me, but I would like to see some of those *kalong* plates you mentioned in your letter. I'd like to have some for my shop.'

'I'll take you to see some tomorrow,' said Leonard. 'You'll know if they're genuine, won't you?'

'Not so sure about that. Pottery can be very deceptive.'

'Like the Thais.'

42

Neville had an urge to tell someone about his encounter with the little drag queen. While in the hotel lobby with Peter waiting for his mother and Jennifer – they were going to the cemetery with flowers – he told him about his experience on the previous evening. 'I picked up what I thought was a girl last night by Tapae Gate, and the creature turned out to be a boy.'

'There are a lot of those about,' explained Peter. 'They are called *kathoi*. They make up and dress in female clothes and live the lives of women more or less. They can be dangerous, especially when in groups.'

'How, dangerous?'

'Demand money at the point of a knife, pick your pocket, that sort of thing.'

'Mine was young, a boy. He didn't seem dangerous. I must say he was quite cunning. He disguised his real sex very cleverly. Even in bed. But I suspected something and found out the truth. I showed my anger. He cowed.'

'You were lucky. You might have been knifed. Not all *kathoi* are bad, of course. There are often a few in villages, and usually they are accepted, but not always. The Thais are tolerant on the whole.'

'Would Arthit be called a *kathoi*?'

'Heavens no! Just gay, or half gay, bisexual. Many Thais are bisexual.' Peter looked at the lifts. 'Here come your mother and Jennifer.' He went up to Barbara.

'Good morning, Peter.'

'I've got some flowers. They're in the boot of my car.'

'You are kind. Shall we go, then?' She turned to Jennifer, who was talking to her brother. 'Come along, let's go.'

Part Two

1

In Tokyo Matthew Bennet put on a white shirt, a blue and red striped tie of sober hue and a dark-blue suit. Most Japanese men possessed a black suit that served for weddings and for funerals, a white tie for the former, a black one for the latter. Matthew had not bothered to get a black suit, thus exercising his unwritten right as a foreigner not to conform with Japanese conventions.

He was dreading the next few hours. Jun, his lover, or ex-lover as he supposed he should now call him, was getting married at Chinzanso, the expensive restaurant and marriage centre. Once the home of an aristocrat, the place had been added on to, thereby depriving it of its traditional Japanese elegance; but the garden remained intact with its waterfall, pond and stream. In it, thousands of photographs had been taken of just-married couples.

Jun had invited Matthew to the Shinto service to be held before the reception, but knowing this to be a private ceremony attended by the family members and the go-between, Matthew had declined. 'But you are more important to me than my family,' Jun had said. 'Better not to have a foreigner there,' Matthew had replied. Matthew had avoided meeting Jun's family throughout their affair. He was embarrassed to do so. 'What would they think of me?' Matthew had asked Jun when a meeting had been suggested. 'They think nothing,' Jun had replied. 'They must think something,' returned Matthew. 'They think,' went on Jun, 'you help me with my English. You teach English at a university. I teach English at a school.'

'But why should I have helped you?'

'Exchange,' Jun had said without hesitation. 'I help you with Japanese things.'

Matthew would never know the answer to his question. His presence at the wedding was explained by the pretence that he had met Jun at a teachers' conference – not in a gay cinema as had been the case. Jun had also invited Sylvia.

'Why Sylvia? You hardly know her.'

'It good to have foreign professor. Impressionate my correague.'

Matthew had arranged to meet Sylvia, who had needed much persuasion before she would agree to attend the wedding, at Mejiro Station.

Sylvia was late. Matthew had told her to be there by ten-thirty. It was now ten-forty and she hadn't come. He stood at the exit watching the clock on the other side of the ticket barrier and the constant flow of arriving passengers; there was no need to scan them so carefully; Sylvia's blonde head would stand out like a beacon in a black sea. At last it did, at a quarter to eleven. 'Am I late?'

'Yes.'

'Sorry. It took longer than I thought it would.'

They got into a taxi.

'Is it far?' she asked.

'Ten minutes.'

Sylvia looked smart in a peacock-blue coat and skirt, a white blouse, a string of pearls and black high-heeled shoes. She wore clothes well. It was a warm day in the middle of April so neither of them was wearing a hat.

'Do you know a Japanese called Yuichi Matsumoto?' asked Sylvia.

'No.'

'He's lodging with a Mrs Chadwick, who happens to live in the flat above my mother's in Hove.'

'You told me about him when you returned from England.'

'Did I? I'd forgotten. Anyway, I don't think I mentioned his name.'

Matthew was too worried about the immediate future to be interested in what Sylvia was saying.

'I met him when I was home,' went on Sylvia. 'He's very attractive, sexy. He told me he'd lived with an English woman in London, Jennifer something, and had also been to bed with her mother; and he was befriended by a millionaire, who helped him; in return for "services", I wondered.'

'Why should he boast to you about his conquests? You must have encouraged him. Anyway, I'm not interested.'

'I thought you would be amused to hear how some Japanese get on in England.'

'I'm not in the mood to be amused by gossip about people I don't know. I'm feeling very sad, as if my life had come to an end.'

'Sorry, Matthew.'

They were silent for a few moments.

'Should I have worn a hat?' asked Sylvia.

'No. The Japanese women won't. Some of them will be in kimono. By the way, I've brought you a special envelope.' He took out of his breast pocket two envelopes decorated with golden characters and a red cord.

'What for?'

'For you to put your gift in.'

'My gift? You said I needn't bring a gift.'

'Each guest has to present one of these envelopes with money in it.'

'How much?'

'For you, five thousand yen would be enough. I must give more. Twenty thousand.'

'Five thousand yen? That's about thirty pounds,' Sylvia objected; nevertheless, she took a five thousand yen banknote out of her handbag and slipped it into the envelope. 'I do call this a swizz.'

Matthew laughed as much at her use of the outdated word as at her attitude. 'The Japanese are practical. The money helps pay for the wedding, which costs the earth.'

After Matthew and Sylvia had presented their gift envelopes to a young man sitting at a table and signed their names in a book, they joined a slow-moving queue at the entrance to one of the banqueting rooms in the Chinzanso complex. Outside the door, the protagonists in the ceremony lined up and bows, followed by words of greeting and congratulations and more bows, had to be made by each guest.

'This queue is inordinately slow,' complained Sylvia quietly to Matthew. 'Why can't they hurry past waving? Should I bow?'

'Yes, but not deeply,' replied Matthew. 'Foreigners look absurd when they try to imitate a Japanese bow.'

Sylvia, when her turn came, gave a slight bow and said 'Congratulations!' to an old bald man in morning dress, and then moved on. Matthew did the same. Next to the old man were two middle-aged couples, the parents of the bride and groom, the men in morning dress, the women in dark kimonos. And then there were Jun and his bride. Sylvia gave her slight bow and smiled and said 'congratulations' again. Matthew did not smile. He looked at Jun in amazement. The young man seemed to have gone through some transfiguration. He was barely recognisable: hair sleek instead of tousled, face like paper, eyes staring and liquid, lips pursed, and his ill-fitting morning dress made him look as unreal as a model in a shop window. Matthew said nothing, but he did bow and the couple returned his gesture, but without giving any sign of recognition. All he noticed about the bride was that she was wearing a gorgeous kimono and round her glossy wig, stuck with lacquer hairpins, was a white bridal band; her face was painted white. 'I've lost him forever,' Matthew sobbed to himself as he joined Sylvia.

They were conducted to places in the middle of a long table; there were three of these stretching down the room from the top table, which was placed across it. Matthew sat opposite

Sylvia. Both were next to Japanese who couldn't speak English. Matthew, wondering who had done the *placement*, spoke a few words in halting Japanese to his neighbours: on his right was a middle-aged woman in a dark kimono which matched her severe regard, and on his left was an elderly man in black suit and white tie who presented him solemnly with his visiting card. Sylvia nodded to her neighbours, smiling vaguely, and then threw a helpless look at Matthew. The table was not too wide so remarks could be passed across it; in any case English utterances would not have been understood. A long pause ensued – 'Photographs,' said Matthew. 'And with the family' – before the Master of Ceremonies, a small bossy, bespectacled man in a dinner jacket stood at a rostrum at the side of the top table and made an announcement in an excited, bombastic voice. Everyone rose when the wedding march from *Lohengrin* played through the amplifiers. Then the bald old man who had been standing in the reception line, the bride and bridegroom and the two fathers entered and took their places at the top table. Jun and his wife, their faces as expressionless as those of marble busts, looked more funereal than joyful.

Waiters served soup. 'Consommé,' said Matthew across the table to Sylvia. 'It always is.' White wine was poured. 'Japanese,' said Matthew, 'Jun ought to have known better.' The Brandenberg concerto which pleasantly accompanied the eating of the soup ceased and the MC spoke into the microphone. The bald old man left the top table, made his way to the rostrum and began to speak. 'He must be the go-between, the *nakodo*,' said Matthew. The speech went on into the next course, steamed swordfish in a white sauce. The guests paid more attention to their food than to what was being said. Then followed other speeches by male and female guests which continued even when Jun and his bride left the table to much camera flashing. 'They're going,' remarked Sylvia to Matthew. 'They'll be back,' he replied, and shortly they returned: Jun in a dinner jacket and the bride in a white evening dress. They had changed their clothes but not their solemnity.

Suddenly Matthew heard his name being called out by the MC: 'Professor Bennet, please.' 'Oh Lord,' muttered Matthew to himself. 'I knew this would happen.' Reluctantly he rose and went to the rostrum. He began with '*O-medito gozaimas.*' His using the Japanese word for congratulations caused the guests to stop their chatter; some clapped. 'I wish Mr and Mrs Sakamoto all happiness in the future.' Matthew glanced at the couple whose faces remained impassive; neither regarded him. 'I have known,' he went on in English, 'Jun-san for some years.' The buzz of talk among the guests started up again. 'And he has become a great friend. A foreigner in Japan needs a helper and this foreigner was very lucky to find such an excellent one in Jun-san. Being illiterate in Japanese meant that half the letters – mostly bills!' – he paused for a laugh that didn't come – 'I received I could not read. I didn't know whether they were invitations, bank statements or demands for payment, until Jun kindly interpreted them for me' – since no one was listening he cut short his speech – 'and he helped me in other ways. My best wishes to the happy pair.' He hurried back to his place. Sylvia was then invited to speak. She hesitated and then, obeying Matthew's 'Go on, just a few words', she went to the rostrum and, looking quite glamorous in her peacock-blue outfit, simply said, 'I sincerely wish Jun and his bride every happiness,' and those few words, probably because of her striking appearance, won a round of applause. Then followed speeches by a few other guests and finally the fathers, which went on well past the fillet steak, the red wine (French), the salad, the ice cream and the coffee.

Pewter candlesticks were placed at the ends and the middle of each table and presently, accompanied by the movement from Mendelssohn's 'A Midsummer Night's Dream', Jun, holding a lighted candle, and his bride visited the unlit candles, bowing and then lighting them with his candle. This quaint ceremony was carried out with the utmost seriousness. When Jun and his bride arrived at the candle near Matthew, Matthew moved aside to allow Jun to reach the unlit candle more easily. 'I love you,' he whispered into Jun's ear. The bridegroom's face retained its stoniness.

While the candle ceremony was proceeding, a five-tiered wedding cake was set on the top table. On his return to his place Jun was handed a large knife by the MC, and, his bride's hand on his, he cut as directed into the bottom tier of the cake. The guests stood and applauded. 'The rest of the cake is cardboard,' said Matthew to Sylvia.

Jun and his wife bowed several times in different directions and left the room. Cameras flashed. The guests resumed their seats.

'That's it,' explained Matthew.

'We don't see them off?'

'No.' Matthew poured some more wine into his glass from a nearby bottle. Laughter and loud voices belonging to a group of young guests started up and so did Japanese pop music.

Matthew and Sylvia rose, after looking at each other and nodding, and bowing vaguely to no one in particular left the room; on their way out a waiter presented each of them with a carrier bag containing something flat.

'What's this?' asked Sylvia.

'Every guest gets a present.'

Outside there was no sign of the departure of the newly-weds.

'What a funny wedding,' said Sylvia in the taxi. 'Poor Jun looked so awful. Is he ill? He seemed in a daze. Drugged, d'you think?'

'Just nervous and anxious to get through with it without mishap.'

'Not a smile out of either of them. One would have thought they'd been sentenced to death by firing squad at dawn tomorrow.'

'Weddings are serious ceremonies in Japan. The bride and groom rarely smile. They are overawed.'

'Overawed? They looked as if they were facing imminent disaster. I wonder if they'll smile on their honeymoon.'

'I wonder,' said Matthew, ruefully. 'They're going to Guam, like thousands of Japanese honeymooners.'

'What have they given us?' said Sylvia, pulling the gift out of the carrier bag. She tore off some of the wrapping and looked inside. 'It's a tray. Looks like a lacquer one. It'll come in handy. I need a tray. At least they didn't give us a doll.'

'I told Jun to give the guests something useful.'

'It must have cost quite a lot.'

'More than five thousand yen, perhaps.'

Before going their separate ways at Mejiro Station, Sylvia said sweetly, 'Bear up, Matthew. Give me a ring soon.'

After swallowing, Matthew rejoined, 'See you at your goodbye party at the university.'

'It's funny to have it after I've left.'

'It's a matter of deciding a date, and consensus,' said Matthew.

2

In spite of the fact that Professor Suzuki had engineered Sylvia's dismissal from the university – there was no definite proof of this but she and others were sure of it – the vindictive, bespectacled, pale little professor was in evidence at the farewell party for Sylvia. It was a lunch-time affair held in the reception room of the Guest Lodge. Armchairs had been pushed against the walls and two long tables bearing cold dishes were placed in the middle of the room.

Sylvia arrived with Matthew. They sat in two of the armchairs. The other faculty members gradually appeared and soon the room was filled, several members having to stand.

Professor Suzuki rose and said in very passable English, 'This is a sad and sorry occasion. We had hoped we would have been able to keep Mrs Field for the three years of her contract, but, alas, owing to the economies the faculty has been compelled to make, we cannot. We must cut our clo-*thes*, our clothes, according to our coats' – Matthew stifled a guffaw – 'unfortu*nate*ly. We shall all miss the sight of that neat blonde head passing through the sea of black heads on the campus, and I personally will miss the sound and valuable advice Mrs Field has given me. Please come again, *mata dozo*.' Suzuki bowed towards Sylvia and sat down to a smattering of applause which mainly came from the Suzuki faction in the department.

'God, what a hypocrite,' murmured Sylvia.

The lukewarm reception was due, Matthew thought, to Suzuki's unpopularity, to the uncomprehension of the speech or the pangs of hunger in the stomachs of the Faculty members, who wanted to tuck into the spread on the tables in the middle of the room.

Kind, gentle Professor Maeda, the chairman of the English Department, who should have spoken first and would have done if Suzuki had not pushed himself forward, rose, put on his reading glasses, took a scrap of paper out of the pocket of his tweed jacket and read in a hesitant accent, 'Mrs Field will be missed, not only by Professor Suzuki but by her students to whom she has won an unforgettable place in their hearts. I know this to be so. She has without complaining given up much extra time to them, especially to the MA candidates, helping them with their thesis. It is very regrettable that she has to go, and I feel ashamed that her contract cannot be honoured. It is good that she is not leaving Japan. From April she will now work for Noguchi Publishing Company. Our loss has been their gain.' He looked up from his piece of paper and said, 'Now let us have a lunch.'

'A good thing you were not asked to speak,' said Matthew to Sylvia.

'I would have refused.'

Matthew looked round the room of guzzling professors. 'I see Suzuki has gone.'

'Have you ever heard such cant? How could he have said all that about missing me when he got me dismissed?'

'Doublefaced.'

'I'll say, I'm going, Matthew. I'll just slip away. See you.' Sylvia left the room. The professors were too busy wolfing their food to notice her departure.

3

Toshi was now living with Sylvia, but he had not given up his apartment in which he spent the night about twice a week, sometimes at the weekends. This annoyed Sylvia. It made her envious and suspicious. What did he do on the nights he slept in his apartment? She asked him once and all he said was, 'I like to be alone sometime.' Was this true? Or did he on these nights meet the doctor's wife at the Club New Love? He had promised to give up this woman, whom Sylvia had seen when she had once gone to the club. The grasswidow, as she might be called, looked a pleasant, motherly female. In exchange for Sylvia's forsaking the greengrocer, the young bank clerk had sworn he would not see the doctor's wife anymore. It had not been difficult for Sylvia to stop her liaison with the greengrocer, who had paid her irregular fleeting visits for a few months, as he seemed to have given her up; frightened off perhaps by Toshi, who had found her *in flagrante delicto* with him. The discovery had been engineered by Sylvia, who, jealous of the doctor's wife, had wanted to show Toshi that she too could be unfaithful.

The scheme had worked. Toshi had stormed out of her flat following an ugly exchange of accusations, but he had returned shortly afterwards and there had been a mutual forgiving. When Sylvia had left for England just before Christmas they had bid each other a loving farewell. Now that Toshi was living with her she became more possessive of him.

It was Toshi who had made the first advance. He had suggested visiting her after she had opened an account at his bank. It was he who, having fallen asleep on the sofa after dinner in her flat, had later stood over her bed, prick rampant. During the following week he had telephoned her constantly. At first she had warded him off, and then slowly visits had begun. He became her lover. In most love affairs love is stronger on one side than on the other. At the beginning love had been stronger on Toshi's side, now it seemed to be stronger on hers. Just as he used to pester her with phone calls, asking where she had been, what she had been doing, she now interrogated him when he returned after she had gone to bed.

'Where have you been?' she asked.

'I been with my correagues. We sing in karaoke bar.'

'You could have telephoned to let me know. I worry when you're late. I have visions of your having an accident and being in the casualty ward of some hospital.'

Toshi was tearing off his clothes in the sitting-room on the other side of the *shoji*, which were half open. Soon he entered the bedroom alcove wearing his vest and his underpants, and hurled himself on top Sylvia, smothering her with violent kisses.

'Oh don't! You stink of whisky.'

He laughed. 'I drink *shochu*.'

'*Shochu* then. Get off.' Through the bedclothes she could feel his ardent prick, a stiff little rod. 'Get off or get in, but shed yourself of that underwear first.'

'Shed? I don't know shed. It a sort of building, I think.'

'It means take off.'

He leapt off the bed, stripped off his vest, kicked off his underpants and slipped between the sheets. He helped Sylvia remove her nightgown and threw it on the floor. He lay on top of her and said, 'English very difficult,' and gave his gurgle of a laugh. She laughed too. 'Darling!' she exclaimed just before his ferocious lovemaking began. To herself Sylvia mused, 'Where else would I find such a lover? This is worth all the worry, all the inconveniences of cohabitation. Aloud she said, 'You're a devil, but I love you.' The climax ended in loud cries of '*Iku, iku!*' from Toshi and moans of delight from Sylvia.

4

Matthew felt bereft. Jun had removed his belongings to his parents' house in Yokohama, where he and his bride were going to live until they had found accommodation in Tokyo. Jun's wife, Midori, did not want to live with his parents. The custom of the son bringing his wife into the family home to become a sort of servant to the mother-in-law was dying. Many a story in Japanese fiction concerned the suffering of the daughter-in-law, especially if there was a suspicion of social inferiority, a Korean connection, or a whiff of scandal such as there being mental instability or hereditary disease in the family. The mother-in-law would often brutally maltreat her son's wife making her go down on her hands and knees and apologise for any shortcomings. In Jun's case this did not happen. His mother was a gentle soul and if perhaps she was jealous of Midori she tried not to show it.

Matthew's flat, though small, felt empty after Jun's departure. He mostly missed his friend in the evening at the hour of his usual return from school. He would listen for the hastening steps on the outside staircase up to the door and the sound of the key in the lock followed by the warm cry, 'Hello-o, I'm back.' And in the morning he missed Jun's hurried yet cheerful preparations: a rich baritone rendition of a Japanese or a Western song from the bathroom, another from the kitchen accompanied by a rattle of dishes. Matthew would lie in bed while Jun washed, dressed, gobbled a bowlful of rice and hastened out of the flat with a 'See you, dear.'

Now all was quiet both in the morning and in the evening, and Matthew was lonely.

Who were his friends in Tokyo?

Apart from Sylvia, there was Bill Cooke, also a teacher, and his friend Minoru, and there were several other American and British gays, some with Japanese chums, others 'single', but none of them was a confidant, except perhaps Bill. Bill, though, possibly because he felt it as the best way to treat Matthew's deprivation, did not lend a very sympathetic ear. 'You had six years,' he reminded Matthew, 'with Jun. You can't expect more. The Japanese have their conventions which they have to follow. You know that.'

'But Jun is gay. Truly gay. He never wanted to marry.'

'You know perfectly well,' returned Bill, impatiently, 'that an only son must marry.'

'It's cruel. As I told you, at the wedding Jun looked as if he were about to be executed. I'm sure he's unhappy. Why doesn't he contact me?'

'He's trying to make a go of it, break away from the old life. He'll get in touch with you in a while, I expect.'

'How long?'

'A year or so, possibly.'

'A year? God! I can't bear not seeing Jun for a whole year.'

'You'd better go to a gay bar and find a substitute.'

'That's what Sylvia said. I don't think that either you or Sylvia understand what love is,' wailed Matthew.

'It's often not much more than a desire to possess.'

'For an American, Bill, you're surprisingly cynical and unromantic.'

'I'm a realist. I stop myself from becoming too emotionally involved. When Minoru graduates and has started a career, I shall understand if he goes his own way. I shall encourage him to. I'm fond of the boy, of course, very much so, but I don't want to disrupt his life.'

'Do you think that I disrupted Jun's life?'

'Sure, of course you did.'

5

Although, like Bill, Sylvia had recommended to Matthew that he find a replacement for Jun, she was more sympathetic than the American. But, Matthew thought, when they were lunching together in her flat, that she was also a bit smug now that Toshi was living with her and Jun was no longer living with him.

'How's the job going?' Matthew asked Sylvia, who had been working at the publishing house for over a month.

'Better than I expected. The boss, as the other employees call him to me, is a decent chap. He's polite and considerate. I don't have to go to the office every day. He lets me work at home, which is what I've been doing this morning.' Sylvia threw a hand in the direction of her desk round the corner from the dining-area in her L-shaped living room. 'It's editing work, which means correcting Japanese English. How appallingly they write our language! Anyway it's more interesting than teaching. Have some more pâté?'

'Thanks.' Matthew helped himself, and, after spreading some pâté over a piece of toast, asked, 'How's Toshi?'

'He's fine. Of course we have our ups and downs. After all, he's twenty-six years younger than I. The age gap – oh dear! How did you manage to bridge it with Jun?'

'I never felt there was such a gap with Jun.' Matthew's eyes watered; he sniffed and ate some more pâté.

'Has be been in touch?'

'No.' He swallowed a sob.

'I'm sorry. I expect he will soon. He's trying to settle down.'

'Not even as much as a telephone call.'

'You must be patient.' Sylvia rose from the table, collected the plates and went behind the curtain that screened the sink and the kitchen appliances. 'I've just got cold chicken and salad,' she announced, emerging with a loaded tray, the present from Jun's wedding.

'Just what I like at lunch time.'

'Toshi doesn't care for an English breakfast. He has rice and any leftovers going. Yesterday he ate the remains of a cottage pie I had made and was counting on for lunch. Fancy cold cottage pie for breakfast! Was Jun the same over breakfast?'

'He'd have rice and pickles.' Again there was a frog in his throat. Sylvia filled his glass with red wine.

'You'll get over it,' she soothed.

'I hope so. At the moment being without Jun is hell. In the evening I still listen for his step on the stairs, his key in the lock.'

Sylvia said, 'I do the same. Sometimes Toshi doesn't come home till after one in the morning. He goes to a karaoke bar, so he says, sings and drinks that *shochu* stuff with his friends. Stinking of alcohol, he throws off his clothes and hurls himself on top of me.'

'Lucky you!'

'Yes, you're right. Lucky me! I wouldn't get a twenty-six-year-old doing that in England. But it won't last. I steel myself for the day when it ends, as end it must. How can it last?'

Matthew helped himself to some more lettuce. 'Your dressing is good, just the right amount of garlic.' After a pause, while he chewed the salad, he said, 'So it's *carpe diem* with you, Sylvia?'

'Exactly. My divorce hardened me, I think. I learnt that one mustn't expect too much of people. One is inclined when one is in love to bestow upon one's lover qualities he doesn't have. I haven't done so with Toshi. He's not much more than a kid, really. But I enjoy his presence, his youthful presence. I won't say he's like a son, not like mine anyway. Mark is gay.'

'Yes, I know. I met him in London with Colin, and when they were here doing those plays.'

'Of course you did. How silly of me not to remember.' Sylvia rose again taking the plates and the salad bowl with her behind the curtain. 'There's a danger,' she said when she reappeared with the cheese dish, on which was a slice of Camembert and another of Emmenthal, and a little basket containing biscuits. 'There's a danger,' she repeated. 'Help yourself, Matthew. The Camembert is local, from Hakodate in Hokkaido.' She spoke to Matthew as if he were new to Japan, when he had been twenty years in the country.

'I know where Hakodate is,' he said grumpily. 'You were saying there's a danger.'

'Yes,' Sylvia helped herself to a piece of Camembert and poured some wine into both the glasses. 'A danger of one becoming over-possessive. And young Japanese men are inclined to take advantage of that. Am I right?'

'Young men anywhere, I should say.'

'And they are inclined to react against this over-possession by not being considerate.'

'By coming in late, for example,' suggested Matthew.

'Yes and other things.'

'It's a mistake to try to stop them from playing their part in Japanese society, from carrying out their obligations.'

'What about Jun?'

'I never kept him on a short leash.'

'Why all this fuss about his marrying?'

'Because it was against his nature to do so and I love him.'

'There's over-possession again.'

'You can call it that if you like,' said Matthew, becoming ruffled.

'Talking of short leashes, I don't keep Toshi on one. But there are limits. Anyway at the moment my relations with Toshi seem to be on an even keel.'

'I'm glad,' said Matthew, crisply.

'This Camembert doesn't taste of anything, does it?'

'I've had better,' said Matthew, dryly.

Sylvia put a hand across the table, palm downwards. 'Dear Matthew. I can see you are miserable. I feel for you, really I do. It'll pass. It'll come right.'

'How?' Matthew put a hand on top of hers for a brief moment.

'I don't know, but I'm sure it will. He'll fade out. Someone else will enter your life, or he'll come back to you.'

'You sound like a fortune teller.'

Part Three

1

In Thailand the searing heat of the hot season begins to make itself felt in March. Chiang Mai lies in a bowl and breezes are infrequent. The fronds of the palms and the dark-green pointed blades of the mango trees are as still as the foliage of an indoor plant; the delicate leaves of the banana tree no longer flap like elephant's ears.

Leonard usually left Chiang Mai at the end of February, but this year he decided to postpone his departure, partly because of Jennifer Lane, who had rented one of the houses belonging to the hotel. The houses were in a lane behind the hotel and were joined, terrace fashion. Before Wilson had left for London he had discovered the existence of this accommodation and had told Jennifer, who intended to stay on because of Somsak, and she had rented one of the houses. Leonard was at first annoyed with Wilson for arranging Jennifer's move to the Golden Plaza, but on meeting Jennifer again Leonard had relented and adopted an avuncular attitude towards the 'western damsel', as he called her to himself and to Wilson; in fact he was lonely, but it was better to be in Thailand than in damp, dark, chilly London. His routine didn't change: he rose late, spent the rest of the morning under an umbrella by the pool with the *Bangkok Post*, lunched in the Coffee Shop or by the pool and then had a siesta, after which, being at a loss for something to do, he would go for a short walk to Fitness Park and on his way back call on Jennifer at around five-thirty, and soon they became friends. Somsak would not appear until about seven – he had evening classes – and before that hour Leonard would tactfully withdraw.

Jennifer would sometimes join Leonard at the pool, but he made it clear to her that he did not wish to be disturbed from his perusal of the newspaper, which he read after his swim. At times he found Jennifer's youthful cheeriness trying. He was curious, though, about her affair with Somsak and it was his curiosity about its development that was the main reason for cultivating her company.

2

When Barbara and Neville had returned to England, Jennifer felt wonderfully free, and when she moved into the house behind the Golden Plaza she was enthusiastic, even though it was not up to much; it was better than Somsak's shack. It had a geyser in the bathroom that roared and snorted alarmingly, but it did produce hot water, while Somsak only had a pitcher into which he dipped a ladle and poured cold water over his body. In spite of this unsatisfactory way of washing Somsak was always clean and never smelled unpleasant.

Somsak would visit her on most evenings. They would have a drink – he a soft one (he, who had drunk so much when she had first met him just after Christmas, had given up alcohol during her absence from Thailand for a reason he had not explained), and she a Mekong whisky with soda and a squeeze of lime (a drink Leonard had told her about); and then they would dine, usually in one of the Thai restaurants in the vicinity. Jennifer wasn't much of a cook and Somsak preferred Thai food to her omelettes or fried chicken and boiled vegetables, so they went out. At the end of the meal there was a pause. Somsak would examine the bill closely and then put it down on the table as if like a contract it required consideration; he would then sigh and get out his wallet, whereupon Jennifer would say, 'No, Somsak, let me pay.' And he did after saying 'No' twice.

That mouth-burning spice, the chilli, was a problem for Jennifer when she was first faced with a Thai dish. Thais like their food laced with chillies, which can be red, green or black. A harmless-looking soup, such as chicken in coconut milk, would have floating in it little black specks that resembled bits of mushroom; in fact they were chillies in their black form. As all foreigners do, Jennifer had tried a dish with chillies in it and suffered; her mouth felt as if it had been stung by a wasp, her eyes watered, her cheeks reddened. Somsak had laughed. Angrily Jennifer had exclaimed, 'It's all very well to laugh. I'm in agony.' Somsak had laughed some more.

Different tastes in food are often the cause of ruptures in a relationship between people of another race, another culture. Somsak, Jennifer thought, should have warned her. it was insular of him to assume she would find palatable what he did. At length, they came to a compromise: Somsak would order two chilli-filled dishes for himself, and three chilli-free dishes for both of them to share.

'*Mai pet,*' Somsak would say to the waiter, meaning 'not spicy'. The first time he said this, Jennifer had laughed. 'I am your pet, darling, not the waiter,' she had said. Somsak had looked confused, and he had not seemed to understand Jennifer's explanation. The Thai for chilli is *prik* and Somsak saying the word had again amused Jennifer. '*Mai prik,*' he had said to the waiter.

'What on earth are you saying?' asked Jennifer.

'*Prik* – it mean chilli.'

'In English it means "cock".' She knew he understood the word. He found her earthiness shocking rather than funny. Somsak, Jennifer slowly discovered, was quite a prude. In the bedroom he would cover his genitals with a hand when he had taken off his underpants, and he looked disapproving when she ran naked into the bathroom. In bed he was exciting, but not for long; he came too quickly. This speedy lovemaking was not satisfying. She put up with it, just as she tolerated his going back to his shack on his motor-scooter afterwards. 'Why can't you live with me?' she once complained to him.

'I mus' go back my school.'

'But why?'

'They give me my room free. If I not there maybe they take it away. And there is my dog, my cat and my chickens. I mus' feed them. What they do without me?'

'Are they more important to you than me?'

Somsak frowned in puzzlement. 'Uh?'

'I love you. You love me?'

'Yes.'

'Yes, what?'

'I love you.' His fine dark eyes did not look at her.

'I think you love your dog, your cat and your chickens more than me.'

'Yes, I love my animal. I love all animal. They need me. My dog he wait outsi' my door; when I go home he very happy. An' my cat he come to me and put his body round my leg.'

'You dog wags his tail, I suppose, and your cat purrs. I'm sorry I haven't a tail to wag and I can't rub my body against your leg.'

The frown of incomprehension fell upon Somsak's face again. 'Uh?'

'Never mind.'

This conversation took place after one of their, for her, unfulfilled sessions upstairs in her large double-bed. He never wished to linger and would hurry to the bathroom. She would follow him and before she was out of the shower he would be downstairs in the living-room sitting in one of the uncomfortable armchairs smoking and leafing through the Sunday supplement of the *Bangkok Post* or some out-of-date magazine. She would give him a Coca-Cola and herself a Thai whisky or a gin and tonic.

'Why will you never have a drink now?' she asked him not for the first time. 'You drank wildly when we first met.'

'I decide it bad for me.' And that was all the explanation she got.

'I admire your strength of will. Where shall we eat tonight?'

'Up to you.'

'But this is your town, Somsak. You know it better than I. You decide. You take me somewhere.'

'You like Kaiwan?'

'We were there last night,' she objected. 'Can't we go somewhere else?'

'What abou' "Khrua Thai"?'

'That fish place?'

'Yes.'

'Don't fancy it somehow tonight.'

Silence. Somsak stared at the dimly lit veranda. Jennifer, frustrated, at last said, 'I'll cook something here.'

'You have rice?'

'No.'

Silence again. Jennifer rose, went into the kitchen and poured herself a strong gin and tonic. 'Another Coca-Cola?' she called out.

'No, thank you.'

No word was exchanged while Jennifer consumed her drink. Somsak lit another cigarette and kept waving at the smoke after each puff.

'I don't mind the smoke,' Jennifer insisted, petulantly. 'One would think it was against the law the way you hide your cigarette between sucks.'

'Suck?' he repeated the word in surprise. She laughed. She knew he was thinking of fellatio. She had told him the word 'suck' was used for such a diversion. 'Let's go to Kaiwan then,' she said. 'It's near and the police are getting strict about helmets; also, we won't have to ride through the stinking traffic. We would if we went to "Khrua Thai".'

Somsak put on his frown of puzzlement. Jennifer realised that he understood less than half of what she said. When she first met him the semi-comprehension hadn't mattered as she had only seen him for a few passionate encounters when language had not been necessary, but now it was beginning to irk her and make her impatient.

In a half-hearted attempt to learn Thai Jennifer bought a little book entitled *Thai Conversation*. It wasn't much help, but it caused a laugh or two nevertheless.

The following made the language sound easy: 'There is no grammar in Thai. No inflections to denote tenses. No Active nor Passive Voice. All is done by special words added to the sentence. There is no singular or plural. No feminine, nor masculine. All is done by mere words added.'

But then came the tones. There were five of them and many homophones. There were no less than six words spelt *mai* in Roman letters and each of them had a completely different meaning. *Mai* could act as a question word, or mean not, mile, new, burn or silk depending on how it was pronounced. Also the book said, 'Apart from the 44 consonants (many of which have the same sound) there are twelve more simple vowels, some of which are placed on top of the consonants.' When Jennifer read this, she sighed in despair. This warning made her laugh: 'It is sometimes shocking to hear foreigners speak Thai because they have imitated the language of their servants. Never make your servants your language teachers.'

The hotel provided a maid who tidied and cleaned the house, but Jennifer had never thought of asking this village girl to give her a lesson. She passed the time of day with her using the greeting, '*Sawatdee-ka*.' And apart from '*Sabai dee ka?*' (how are you?) that was all.

She liked to stroke Somsak's beautiful black locks, but after reading, 'The head is considered a very high and sacred thing. you should never touch nor pat anyone's head. It is considered a gross insult. Do not jump over someone's head.' 'I've never done that, at least,' Jennifer smiled to herself. Somsak had not protested when she had stroked his hair; perhaps the regulation didn't apply to lovers in bed together.

3

'What about learning Thai?' Jennifer asked Leonard during one of his evening visits.

'Oh I shouldn't bother, if I were you. It's a difficult language, especially the pronunciation.' Leonard took a cigar out of his shirt pocket. 'You don't mind, do you?'

'No, please go ahead. Somsak asked me who had been here the other day when he smelt cigar smoke. I told him you'd been here. He seemed a bit suspicious.'

Leonard laughed. 'They are terribly suspicious, and superstitious too. D'you know they give their children nicknames because they fear that if the evil spirits knew their real ones they might harm them? They believe in spirits. That's why they have spirit houses outside their homes: to pacify the evil spirits and to please the good ones. They put rice and fruit in the spirit house. You may have noticed.'

'Yes I have. In some ways it's good to believe in spirits, I think; after all, we talk about luck. But to go back to what I was saying. I learn a Thai word and when I say it I'm not understood.'

'They think you're speaking English,' explained Leonard. 'They don't listen.'

'How do you say money in Thai? It's spelt *n-g-e-r-n* in the dictionary I've got.'

'I think,' replied Leonard, 'But I may well be wrong, that you should forget the "g" and say *nern*. You're not seriously thinking of learning Thai, are you?'

'I'd like to communicate better with Somsak. At the moment we often speak at cross purposes, not understanding one another, or only half understanding. He doesn't seem all that interested in learning English. He's no linguist, nor am I, come to that.'

Leonard laughed again. 'You remind me of those couples who sit by the pool: he elderly, Western; she a Thai floozie with no English, or just a smattering. Hardly a word passes between them. They've nothing in common. One hears the foreigner say, "You like drink?" "Yes, I like," she replies. "What you like?" "I like Coca-Cola and ice cream." At meals the waiter often knows more English than the girl, and may be asked to interpret. Again silence, apart from a few "You-likes" and "Yes-I-likes". At least the language of love needn't be expressed in words. A wide vocabulary is not required.'

'It's not quite as bad as that with Somsak and me.'

'I didn't suppose it was. What are you plans?'

'To stay on here.'

'It gets awfully hot, you know.'

'I know. What about a drink? Have some of your whisky.'

Leonard had given her a bottle of Scotch, which she kept for him. In her desire to be like a Thai she often drank Mekong whiskey with fresh lime and soda, not a drink a Thai woman would have, but being from the West, Jennifer needed an alcoholic stimulant in the evening. She crossed the stone floor of the large living-room which ran the length of the house and in the kitchen poured out a Scotch for Leonard and a Mekong for herself.

'I know it gets hot. It's hot enough already.' She handed Leonard his drink. 'But what am I to do? I've burnt my boats. I've let my flat in London. I gave up my job. I certainly don't want to be with my mother at Grasslands, the family home, which she has put up for sale anyway. I want to be with Somsak.'

'Does he want to be with you?'

'Good question – how I hate that expression! One finds oneself using terms one despises. Does he want to be with me?

He comes round most evenings. He told me once that he couldn't spend the night here because of his dog, his cat and his chickens; so I'm rated pretty low, I guess. Anyway he does come round and often, not always, we go to bed, but—'

'But what?'

'There's a problem. May I tell you?'

'Please do,' said Leonard eagerly, leaning forward in his chair whose wooden bar had been digging into his back.

'He—. I hope you don't mind my saying this. I sort of feel I can to you because you're, you're er—'

'An old queen? An elder sister?'

'No, not that but I feel I can confide in you. One needs to confide in someone.'

'And there being no female available, the next best thing is an old poof.'

'No, Leonard. It's just that you're cosy. I feel I can say things to you I couldn't say even to my mother.'

'I could never tell my mother anything, but then I had something to hide.'

Jennifer tossed back her drink, screwed up her nose, put down her glass, braced herself and gabbled out, 'He comes too quickly.'

'Ah, premature ejaculation,' said Leonard. 'Many men suffer from it. King Farouk did, and so did—'

'What am I to do? He lies on top of me and as soon as he enters he comes.'

'Hmm.' Leonard put the tips of his fingers together and pursed his lips. 'There's one thing you can try: let him lie back and then, after a while, say half an hour, make him do it again. The second time should be better. At his age – how old is he?'

'Thirty-two.'

'A mere boy. He should be able to perform two or three times.'

'But he doesn't want to. As soon as he's finished he leaps out of bed and runs to the bathroom. And when he comes back wearing just a towel round his waist – he looks so handsome – and not properly dry, he starts to dress. He doesn't seem to understand that I need satisfying.'

'Thai men can be selfish,' said Leonard knowledgeably.

'Is there anything I can do?'

'Ply him with drink. That should slow things up.'

'But he's given up alcohol. I must say he was better at it when he drank. He did when I first met him.'

'Can't you persuade him to go back on to the bottle?'

'No. He's very determined about it.'

'Get some pot and smoke it together. That might retard the climax.'

'I don't know how to get any.'

'He will. Ask him. Does he smoke?'

'Yes, but I've given up. I used to smoke pot at university and at London parties it was the thing. I gave up cigarettes and pot at the same time. And there's something else.'

'Oh? And what's that?' asked Leonard, interested.

'He sniffs my body. He puts his nose to my cheek, my breasts, my stomach and sniffs.'

Leonard laughed. 'It's the Thai way of kissing. It excites him to sniff you.'

'I don't like it. It's as if he were testing to find out if I'd washed.'

'No, no. It's not that at all. It's a sign of affection.'

'Whatever it is it makes me squirm.'

'You must get used to it. Love in the East is different, like their conception of the truth.'

4

Group tourists spend on average two nights in Chiang Mai and then they may be taken on to Chiang Rai and the Mekong River to goggle at the view of the confluence of the River Ruak and the Mekong, a tongue of Burma and across the great waterway the wooded hills of Laos. The view is called the Golden Triangle. 'Triangle' because one can see three countries from it, and 'golden' because in the distant wooded hills the opium poppy is cultivated and refined into heroin, the source of many fortunes and many money-laundering operations. The tight programme keeps the tourists busy; they've no time to be bored. Winter visitors, like Leonard, had a lot of time on their hands and were often at a loose end. The strangeness of the place had worn off; no longer was Leonard surprised or amused by Thai customs, manners or simple extortionate tricks. His late rising, his gentle swim, his sitting by the pool with the newspaper, over the top of which he would appraise the swimmers and the sunbathers, his gin and tonic and salad lunch made the morning pass pleasantly; then came his siesta, his stroll, and then at five-thirty his visit to Jennifer. The evenings were a problem. He disliked dining alone – he gobbled his food when he was by himself – nor did he fancy going to bed directly after eating. What was he to do? On some evenings he would sit in the hotel lounge reading or watching the international news on television; on others he would go to one of the gay bars – he had given up trying to make Jim of Jim's Bar in the Night Market. When in a gay bar he would never engage the services of any of the bar boys; he would watch with amusement and a certain amount of pleasure their little bodies jogging in pointless go-go antics, and ward off their feigned amorous advances by buying them drinks knowing full well they got a percentage of the price of each beer or soft drink imbibed.

One of the bars put on a rape sketch, which Leonard found hilarious. A boy wearing shirt, trousers, jacket, tie and a baseball cap, wandered on to the little stage. Suddenly he was assaulted by three boys in G-strings who tore off his clothes and while two of the boys held him down, the third pretended to enter his 'back door', as the Thais would say euphemistically. The victim's screams brought a policeman on to the scene, but he, instead of arresting the culprits, lowered his trousers, pushed the third boy out of the way and took his place. More screams summoned a 'doctor' who ordered the policeman to cease. He then shed his white coat, under which he was wearing nothing. After examining the 'back door', he entered it himself. The sketch ended in all the 'actors' dancing round and having a pretence gang-bang and grinning broadly.

On some mornings Leonard hired a *tuk-tuk* to take him into the centre of the town. Holding a handkerchief to his large nose because of the polluted air, Leonard would be whisked through the traffic at a speed he didn't at all enjoy; still less did he enjoy the clouds of poisonous fumes that belched from exhausts when the vehicle was stationary at traffic lights. On arrival at the head of Tapae Road opposite the reconstructed Tapae Gate, he would alight, pay the driver, and stroll up the main street of Chiang Mai. He would have no purpose in mind; the little outing simply made a change in his routine. One morning he stopped to look at a plate of bananas which, oddly, stood on a table outside an antique shop. He glanced round and saw a young man sitting in the next shop and staring at him. The young man held up his thumb in a suggestive manner and smiled. Leonard went across to him. 'You li' bananas?' he asked the Englishman.

'Er, yes,' replied Leonard, wondering if there was a double meaning in the question.

'Where you stay?'

'Golden Plaza.'

'You li' I bling to *you*? How abou' five o'clock?'

'OK. I'll meet you in the lobby.'

'How you go back?'

'*Tuk-tuk.*'

'*Tuk-tuk* expensive. Why you no take bus?'

'Too slow.' Leonard looked at his new acquaintance. He had small, brown hooded eyes and his nose was flat and broad at the nostrils. 'No beauty,' Leonard remarked to himself, 'but charming. He'd be no trouble.' Aloud he asked, 'What is your name?'

'Amnuay.'

At ten minutes to five Leonard was waiting, a little self-consciously, in the lobby of the Golden Plaza, and at five o'clock precisely Amnuay arrived bearing in his arms four hands of bananas. Embarrassed, Leonard, watched by the bellboys, greeted his banana-loaded friend. 'Heavens, so many!' he exclaimed.

'You say you li' banana.' Amnuay's nose flattened as his mouth turned upwards to form a generous smile.

They ascended in the lift to the fourth floor, and when the doors opened Amnuay hesitated. Standing by the lift was one of the chambermaids with a trolley piled with bed linen. Amnuay spoke to her for a few moments and then accompanied Leonard to the bedroom. As soon as he had put the consignment of bananas on the large double-bed, he threw himself into Leonard's arms and said, 'I li' you. I no can stay. She my cousin from my village. Maybe she tell my wife.'

'Oh dear! What did you say to her?'

'I say I bling your order of banana and I fix up your trekking plan. I work in trekking office. I mus' go. I telephone you.' He gave Leonard a wet kiss and hurried out of the room.

Leonard looked at the four clusters of bananas and laughed. 'What am I going to do with them? Trekking! Can the maid believe I eat as many bananas as an elephant and go trekking?' He sat on the armchair and roared with laughter.

5

The next day after at five-thirty he paid his customary call on Jennifer, bearing with him two of the four hands of bananas.

'I thought you'd like these,' he said.

'So many! How can I eat all these?'

'Perhaps Somsak will help you. I have a big supply.' Leonard told Jennifer about Amnuay, his gift of bananas and his cousin. He could be frank with her and she had confided in him about Somsak's disability.

'I'm going to be your neighbour, Jennifer.'

'What?'

'I've taken the house next to yours. Amnuay has made an impression. I want him to be able to visit me without his running into a relation.'

'It isn't like you to stay in such austere quarters. You live in such grandeur in London.'

'Without an Amnuay.'

'You had Trevor and Yuichi,' Jennifer reminded him, rather spitefully. She rose from the springless sofa and went to the kitchen to pour drinks. On her return, she said, 'I sometimes think of Yuichi, do you?' She handed him his whisky. 'He was a cunning bastard, getting what he could out of people. He's with my great aunt in Hove, exploiting the old crone, I bet. I'm glad I broke up with him, even though I apparently wrongly accused him of having it off with Trevor. He double-crossed me over you. All the same I do think of him sometimes. A little shit, but maddeningly exciting, wickedly so somehow.'

Leonard sipped his drink. After a pause he said, 'He is a satyr, a sensualist blessed or cursed with the devilish art of lovemaking. He knew how to gratify one.'

'Devilish art! That's right. I wish that—' She stopped herself from saying what she had in mind.

Leonard, though, guessed. 'You wish that Somsak was a bit like him?'

'No, no. I don't. Somsak is a sweet man, not in the least calculating.'

'Did you try the pot.'

'Yes.'

'Did it work?'

'Not really. After a while we got the giggles and when we

tried to make love we laughed, which is hopeless as you probably know. We then fell asleep and when we woke up we felt too listless to do anything.'

'You'd better try *ya maa*.'

'What is that? Some Thai herbal stuff?'

'No, amphetamines.'

Part Four

1

It was June, a wet and depressing month in Japan when shoes become mouldy. It was over two months since Jun's wedding and Matthew had not heard a word from him. He felt so lonely that he decided to resign from his university post at the end of the academic year which would come to a close the following March. He first told the mild and gentle Professor Maeda of his decision. Maeda at once tried to dissuade him. 'But you have tenure now,' the professor said. 'You can stay till you're sixty-five.'

'I feel I've had enough,' replied Matthew.

'We all feel like that at times, Professor Bennet. We must endure. *Gambatté!*'

'I'm not sure that I want to.'

Maeda said, 'Please think it over. I will tell no one about it.'

Matthew mentioned his plan to Sylvia. 'You're crazy,' she said. 'You'll never get as good a job anywhere else, not as well paid anyhow. What will you do?'

'Lotus eat for a while.'

'Fatal for someone of your age.'

'I'm fifty-six. I could stay on till I'm sixty-five. I don't think I can stick nine years more, Sylvia. How long will you stay?'

'Till Toshi tires of me or he gets married or something.'

'How are things going at the moment?'

'Bumping along, one might say. But I enjoy the bumps; they give edge to my existence, prevent tedium, produce excitement, uncertaintly. Once there is certainty, excitement goes and so does romance.'

'You've been reading *The Importance of Being Earnest*,' said Matthew, after Sylvia's parody of Algernon's lines.

'You mean "the very essence of romance is uncertainty"?' Sylvia laughed. 'You're right and so was Wilde. Professor Suzuki asked me what the line meant once. Do you ever see him?'

'Frequently. He's always polite. He'll be delighted to hear I'm resigning.'

'You're not serious, are you, Matthew?'

2

A few weeks later Matthew, on the prowl in Shinjuku, ran into a young man he had met over a year ago in a cinema. He had forgotten his name but he remembered the expectant drive to a 'love' hotel on the outskirts of Yokohama. The 'love' had been appropriately torrid, but the aftermath had been infuriating: the young man had given Matthew crabs.

'You remember me?' asked the young man.

'Yes,' replied Matthew coldly. 'I've forgotten your name.'

'My name Yamamoto Kazuyoshi.'

'I remember now. You gave me *kejirami*.'

'Not possible.' The young man looked down.

'I suppose you got rid of them.'

'I never. I swear. I no have now. You come with me?'

He was handsome and seemed to be turned on by Matthew. 'He must have got rid of them' thought Matthew. 'He couldn't have allowed their occupation of his crotch for more than a year.' Matthew was attracted. He recalled the thrill of that night in the 'love' hotel.

'You can come back to my place. Nobody there now.'

They drove in Yamamoto's Toyota sports car to Matthew's flat. Once inside they embraced passionately and then hastily tore off their clothes. Matthew held out his arms to ward off another amorous attack. 'I'd better have a look,' he said, like a doctor whose patient has complained of a stomach pain. 'I hope you don't mind.'

'I'm clean,' protested Yamamoto.

'Lie back on the bed, please.'

Yamamoto obeyed. Matthew fetched a torch and a magnifying glass and examined the dark, luxuriant forest. 'You seem to be clear of them,' he announced in a medical tone. The telephone rang. 'Bugger!' Matthew kissed the tip of Yamamoto's erect cock and then went into the sitting-room to answer the call.

'Hello? Jun! At last you ring. Why didn't you ring before?'

'I was trying to be a husband.'

'No good?'

'No good. I rang you many times this evening. Were you out?'

'Yes. Where are you?'

'In Yokohama.'

'Good.'

'I come to see you now?'

'OK. Fine.' It was only ten o'clock and it would take Jun over an hour to get to the flat. 'See you.' Matthew returned to the bedroom and a steamy but hurried session with Yamamoto ensued. But why not? Matthew asked himself. Fortunately Yamamoto didn't wish to stay and it was not long before he drove off. 'Lust goes to Yokohama,' mused Matthew. 'Love comes from Yokohama.' he sat in the sitting-room reading, but not taking in, *The Golden Bowl* (the diffuseness of Henry James made the story difficult to follow when one was in an agitated mood; he kept re-reading the same page) until he heard those dear hasty steps on the outside staircase. Jun arrived out of breath with a knapsack on his back and a suitcase. Repeating the hugs and kisses he had just given Yamamoto, Matthew felt remorseful, but not for long. Jun wished to unburden himself of his marriage woes and did so until the night was almost over.

'You not take another lover?' asked Jun, giving Matthew a wary look.

Wondering if Jun's Japanese sixth sense suspected something, Matthew replied, 'No, not really. I waited for you.' This was more or less true.

3

One evening Toshi returned to Sylvia's apartment on the point of tears.

'They send me away,' he sobbed.

'Who and where? Come and sit down, darling. Have a drink.'

'A whisky,' choked out Toshi.

Sylvia went into the kitchen area and poured out a good measure of whisky for Toshi and a strong gin and tonic for herself. On her return, she found Toshi sitting with his head in his hands. She sat by him on the sofa. 'Here's your whisky, darling.' She put his glass on the coffee table, sipped her drink, and then holding it in her left hand put her right arm round Toshi's shoulders. 'Now tell me what it's all about,' she said maternally.

'They send me away,' sobbed Toshi.

'Who sends you away?'

'My bank. The manager. He have secret man who tell him about us. I must go to Saga.'

'Where's that?'

'Far. Very far. Small town in Kyushu. I told you it danger if I live with you.'

'Why shouldn't you live with me? I can't do you or the bank any harm.'

'They think it bad for me to live with a foreigner.'

'But, Toshi, you're in the Foreign Department.' She removed her arm from Toshi's shoulders and gave him his whisky. 'Drink some of this, dear.' Toshi took a gulp, gurgled, stuck out his tongue and said, 'Very strong.' It was practically neat.

'Why can't you stand up to the manager. Tell him that your private life has noting to do with him.'

'It not possible.'

'Who is this secret man, this spy who's been watching you?'

'I'm not sure.'

'Shall I go and see your manager? I could tell him that your seeing me, your living with me, is actually good for the bank as you're learning English from me.'

'You cannot help me.'

'It's damnable. When will you go?'

'Next week.'

'As soon as that? How long will you have to stay in this place?'

'Maybe two years.'

'God!'

4

The day after Jun's return, Matthew rang Sylvia. 'I've wonderful news,' he told her.

'I wish I had. I've terrible news. Tell me your "wonderful news" first and then I'll divulge what's happened. It's truly dire.'

'Jun's back!' exclaimed Matthew, triumphantly.

'I always thought he'd come back to you.'

'You never said so.'

'Oh yes, I did. Well, my news is that Toshi has been transferred to some remote town in Kyushu. His bank manager set a spy on his tracks and he discovered that Toshi was living with me.'

'I always said it was an unwise arrangement, your living so near the bank.'

'I don't remember your saying so.'

'I did, you know.'

'It's the insular xenophobia the Japanese suffer from. Foreigners contaminate poor little bank clerks, even those in the Foreign Department.' Sylvia gave a bitter laugh. 'It's ridiculous.'

'Let's meet for one of our lunches soon, Sylvia. It's my turn.'

'After Toshi has gone. I want to be with him as much as possible before he leaves; he'll have a few days off. He's moving out of my flat; daren't stay. It's monstrous. But he's keeping on his room, as he calls his apartment in Nerima-ku. I will help him with the rent. He'll be able to fly up here now and then, I hope, and I can meet him in his flat. Let me know about lunch. I won't be much of a guest. I'm miserable.'

'Poor Sylvia!' soothed Matthew.

'Yes, poor Sylvia! And lucky Matthew! Bye.' She rang off.

5

As the sun slowly and relentlessly moved towards the Tropic of Cancer, north of Chiang Mai, the shadows cast by the umbrellas round the pool of the Golden Plaza diminished. Leonard, unlike the tourists from the West, did not enjoy being baked and burnt; he pushed his chair close to the table so it was in the shade. There were fewer tourists; however, there were some white bodies exposed to the fierce ultraviolet rays. Husbands and wives, lone bachelors, Thai hostesses with swains or sexagenarians smeared themselves or each other with suntan cream which permeated the still air with a sickly aroma. Leonard hated the smell. He spent less and less time by the pool, just swimming his ten lengths and glancing at the front page of the *Bangkok Post*. His expensive Panama hat, admired by the pool waiter with the fine legs, was becoming grubby, but when Leonard wore it at an angle he still looked debonair.

He now lunched in his house. He loathed shopping, never having done much of it in his life, so he had something sent over from the hotel, until Amnuay heard of this extravagance and was shocked by it and insisted on providing the ingredients for Leonard's midday meal. The diet, which Amnuay chose, was monotonous: carrots, potatoes and ham, and bananas. In the evening Leonard dined out. His late afternoon visits to Jennifer next door continued.

'You've never let me meet Mr Banana,' she complained to Leonard.

'He's not really *sortable*, you know, not being blessed with many social graces. He doesn't want to meet any foreigners except me. He's shy.'

'I've seen him,' said Jennifer. 'He comes on a motor-scooter, wearing a helmet, around two in the afternoon, doesn't he?'

'That's right. He stopped me from having lunch sent over from the hotel. He does my shopping for me and keeps me on a simple diet. He will buy loaves of white bread which is like blotting paper.'

'There's no need to have that. There's a shop that sells wholemeal bread at the top of the lane.'

'Is there? I must tell him. He told me that all he had for breakfast was sticky rice, every morning. I read somewhere that the Thais like to eat the same dishes every day.'

'They're not very enterprising in the kitchen,' agreed Jennifer. 'I think that Somsak would be content with a bowl or two of steamed rice or noodles laced with chillies. I'm sure he doesn't have much more than that at home.'

'They eat to fill their stomachs, not to savour the taste, not that they can taste anything; their taste buds are wrecked by the chillies they eat. Won't Somsak be having holidays soon?'

'We're planning to go to Krabi on the Andaman sea. One can get a cabin in the hotel grounds. How long will you stay, Leonard?'

'It's getting so hot. I don't know how long I can stand it.'

'You have air coolers that work. I don't. I just have fans.'

'Fans are better. They don't make a noise. When I have my cooling system on it's like being in a helicopter. Thank the Lord the temperature drops at night. One doesn't want to go out much in the day. I go over to the hotel to collect my letters and the newspaper. That's about all, apart from a brief swim. Haven't seen you in the pool recently, Jennifer.'

'I go in the afternoon.'

'Too many screaming kids then. By the way, it's just occurred to me, let's have a dinner party: you and Somsak, me and Amnuay. What about it? I'll get the ingredients. We could have smoked salmon, chicken casserole, cheese and a cake. What about that? And wine, of course. The Thais are beginning to get a taste for wine.'

'Not "our" Thais, surely. I don't think Somsak, who doesn't drink anyway, would care for such a menu,' said Jennifer. 'He won't eat cheese and I shouldn't think he'd like smoked salmon.'

'We're always eating their dishes. Why shouldn't they try ours?'

'I thought your friend only came at two o'clock in the afternoon. We can't dine then.'

'He'll have to make an exception. Go home late for a change. He lives in a village north of Chiang Mai, twenty-five minutes away on his bike, so he tells me. He's married and has a son aged sixteen or seventeen.'

'Heavens!'

'Go for the married ones, a friend once advised me. They're more reliable.' Leonard gave Jennifer a mischievous look.

She laughed. 'Don't their wives mind being deceived?'

'Not so much if it's a man, especially not if it's a foreign man. Thai husbands are notoriously promiscuous, but when they form an attachment to an old man like me they don't mind. The attachment brings money into the household.'

'Do you *pay* Amnuay then?' asked Jennifer in a disapproving tone.

'Oh yes, more than his salary, I should think.'

'Should I pay Somsak?'

'No. Your youth, your sex and your fair complexion, not to mention your blonde hair, are enough payment. By the way did you try the amphetamines?'

'No. He was against them. He doesn't mind *ganja*, as they call pot here, since it comes from a plant. He says amphetamines are dangerous as they are chemical. His students take them and he tries to stop them from doing so.'

'Sensible. When shall we have our dinner party? What about Saturday?'

'That seems as good a day as any. I'll ask Somsak.'

'And I'll ask mine.'

With the help of Amnuay, who managed to get an hour off one morning from his office, Leonard shopped for the party at a nearby supermarket, going there and back in a *tuk-tuk* followed by the helmeted Amnuay on his scooter. 'You will come, won't you?' asked Leonard when the shopping was done and Amnuay was about to return to his office on his bike; he had donned his helmet which made him seem like someone else. Leonard placed a foot in the *tuk-tuk* and glancing round at his friend, said, 'You could stay the night. You've never stayed the night.'

Amnuay, who had started his bike, shouted, 'Okay!', and sped away.

6

'Oh, there's something I've been meaning to ask you,' Sylvia said to Matthew over lunch in Matthew's apartment. It was a Saturday and neither of them had to go to work. Jun had a meeting at his school.

'What's that?' Matthew returned from his kitchen alcove with a platter containing slices of cold pork.

'Why did Jun behave in that very peculiar manner at his wedding?'

Matthew handed Sylvia the dish of pork. 'I did ask him why. He said he was trying to look solemn like a Japanese bridegroom and at the same time he was sad, despondent and a little scared about the future. Help yourself to salad, and there's potato salad too, and Dijon mustard, and apple sauce.'

'Thanks. How extraordinary!' remarked Sylvia, helping herself to salad.

Matthew poured a little of the white Bordeaux into his glass and tasted it. 'It seems all right.' He filled Sylvia's glass and then his. 'It's good that the yen is strong and that wine is now fashionable in Japan.'

'What about the marriage?'

'It didn't work. Simply that.'

'What about her, the wife?'

'She's gone back to her parents. Jun and I are going to England in August. I'm renting an apartment in Garden Mansions, near Sloane Street.'

'Don't make me envious. I shall have to sweat it out here without Toshi. We may meet somewhere in mid-August when there is a festival.'

'O-Bon,' said Matthew, knowledgeably. 'The Festival of the Dead. The dead ancestors are supposed to return as spirits.'

'How jolly!'

'It is jolly as a matter of fact.'

'Of course. I remember now. Toshi and I went to a Shimoda at the time of the festival last year. How silly of me to forget! We danced in a temple yard. It was fun.' Sylvia's eyes watered. 'It's damnable this separation.'

'He might have had to go anyway,' said Matthew, unhelpfully. 'Banks do move their employees around.'

'Saying that is a lot of help.' Sylvia sniffed, getting her handkerchief out of her handbag and blew her nose. 'Sorry,' she said.

'Has Toshi gone?'

'Yes,' replied Sylvia angrily. 'Yes, he has.'

'You have my sympathy. I know what a separation is like.'

7

'Well,' said Leonard to Jennifer, 'it's a quarter to seven.'

They were sitting in Jennifer's house, where the dinner was to take place, and drinking whisky.

'Somsak is sometimes late,' said Jennifer.

'Amnuay is always on time. Perhaps he's held up at the office. I told him I'd be in your house, not mine, so he knows to come here.'

'I have a sort of feeling they won't turn up. I don't think Somsak wanted to. He said he would, but I sensed he didn't want to come to our dinner party.'

'Amnuay seemed pleased with the idea, or I thought he did. Of course one must realise that the Thais hate to disappoint one. They say "yes" in order to please when they really mean "no". But I didn't think Amnuay was like that. Let's have another drink.'

Jennifer rose and replenished the glasses and then resumed her seat on the bony sofa. At around seven-thirty the phone rang. Jennifer jumped up. 'Yes? We've been waiting for you ... what ... why ... oh, all right.' She banged down the receiver. A few minutes later the phone rang again. It was Amnuay. Leonard heaved himself out of his chair. 'Yes? ... oh, hello, Amnuay ... I'm all right, thanks and how are you? Good. Oh, dear, but you said you would. Can't help it? A group? That's unusual isn't it. Unusual, not ordinary, strange, not normal ... yes, that's right ... never mind, *my pen rai*. If you can't, you can't. See you tomorrow. Goodbye.' Leonard laughed. 'Amnuay, as you may have gathered, can't come either. He has to look after a group, take them to the Night Bazaar or somewhere. So we dine alone. No stilted conversations full of misunderstandings. Perhaps it's as well.'

They moved to the dining table at the end of the long room. 'I shall go to England next week, but I'll keep on the house,' said Leonard, picking up a piece of lime and squeezing it over the smoked salmon.

'As I told you Somsak and I are going to Krabi, or we're supposed to be going there.'

'What about the wine?' asked Leonard. 'Did you open it?'

'Yes.'

'Good girl. Let's have it now. It won't go with the smoked salmon, but never mind. I should have got white as well. Stupid of me.'

Jennifer fetched the bottle of claret which Leonard had bought, and poured out the wine without tasting it first.

'I hope it's all right,' said Leonard taking a sip.

'It's not bad. Here's to a happy holiday!'

'If Somsak didn't agree to go with me out of politeness and doesn't really mean to go at all,' said Jennifer, resentfully.

'Oh, I'm sure not,' encouraged Leonard, putting a forkload of smoked salmon into his mouth.

The following week saw Leonard's departure for London, and Jennifer and Somsak setting out for Krabi on the coast of the Andaman Sea. Leonard leavened his farewell to Amnuay, whose happy face became serious and tearful, with a wad of banknotes.

Part Five

1

Gertrude Jenkins was in Winifred Chadwick's apartment in Hove having been invited to tea. Yuichi had gone to London for the day. Gertrude noticed that the old lady's flat was in need of a thorough cleaning; there was dust everywhere. Observing Gertrude's critical glances round the sitting-room, Winifred said, 'I shall have to get a char. Yuichi isn't much good at dusting, but he's a very pleasant companion, far more interesting than Miss Pinnock ever was. Have you heard from your daughter recently, Gertrude?'

'She told me on the phone that she liked her new job in a publishing house, and she intends to stay in Tokyo indefinitely.'

'I wonder how long Yuichi will stay in England,' said Winifred, wistfully. 'What will I do without him? By the way, did I show you the portrait he's painting of me?'

'We were going to see it on that bridge afternoon in my flat, but we never got round to it, d'you remember? I'd love to see it.'

'Then help me up and give me my stick, please.'

Gertrude did so, remarking to herself that Winifred seemed frailer than when she had last seen her. Winifred, clutching pieces of furniture with her left hand and using her stick for support in her right, led the way to the spare room. The painting was covered by a sheet, a palette was on a chair, paint brushes in jam jars were on the floor. 'Now,' said Winifred in a commanding tone, 'remove the sheet from the picture, please, and the palette from the chair – how untidy dear Yuichi is – so I can sit down.'

Gertrude obeyed the instructions and then stood by the old

lady, who seated herself. 'One would have thought,' remarked Winifred, 'that, being Japanese, Yuichi would be neat, but he isn't. Perhaps the Japanese aren't neat. One's ideas about people one doesn't know are often erroneous. Now, don't say what you think yet. Look carefully first.'

Gertrude wasn't much of an art critic. What she saw was a painting of a bad-tempered, spoilt old woman in a long gaudy dress. The pale face contrasted strongly with the violent colours of the strange garment, the fan she was holding and the auburn shawl which matched her wig. It was a striking portrait, recognisable, perhaps cruelly so.

'Well, what do you think?' demanded Winifred.

'It's great,' replied Gertrude, feebly.

'He's made me look such a fright. I know I don't.'

Gertrude searched for something to say. 'It makes you look dominant, an indomitable empress.'

Winifred chortled. 'That's good: "dominant", "an indomitable empress". I suppose I am rather like that. It's not quite finished as you can see. The left hand needs going over. Now, let's struggle to the dining-room, where Yuichi told me he'd laid the tea things. Would you mind putting on the kettle; it's electric and in the kitchen; it's got water in it; it just needs switching on; there's a canister of Earl Grey on the table.' Winifred seemed a little out of breath when she took her seat in the dining-room.

2

Since her return from Thailand, Barbara had been more or less confined to Grasslands. The house had been put on the market, with Neville's approval and to Veronica's dismay, and Barbara felt that she should be in residence in case the estate agent wanted to bring round a prospective purchaser. The gardener or his wife could have shown people round, but Barbara preferred to be present herself when would-be purchasers looked at the house, which was still fully furnished. She had given Henry's clothes to Oxfam and presented his suitcase packed with Japanese and Thai soft-porn gay magazines to Wilson, to his embarrassment. She had done this at Cecily's suggestion, when she, Cecily and Wilson were dining at Neville's Kensington flat. Otherwise she had not got rid of any furniture, ornaments or paintings. She was reluctant to empty the house of its embellishments, of things she had known all her married life, and things she had known as a child which she had brought to Grasslands after her wedding. Her possessions were superior to Henry's. Her crested Georgian and Victorian silver had replaced Henry's plated spoons and forks which had been relegated to the kitchen. Another reason for leaving the place intact was that a house looks better furnished than empty.

There had been several so-called prospective buyers, but when she had shown them over the large Edwardian house and its grounds, she sensed that they were only curious to see what the property was like and were not serious purchasers.

For a reason she could not explain to herself, Arthit often came into her thoughts and she wondered how Henry's Thai friend would spend the fifty thousand pounds he had been left. She wrote to him.

In spite of his limited vocabulary and his ignorance of English syntax, he managed to write a reply that was amusing, unintentionally so, but clearly sincere.

Dear Barbara Lane,
    Your letter come. Thank you. Hello what you doing now. I hope the weather is good now and the flower are blooming and the tree are evergreen. Everything and your health is good and should be strong forever. In Thailand now very hot. We just finish Songkram water festival everyone they throw water at everyone. I like play the water with you.
    My wife she want know when money Henry give me will come. I not want the money. My wife she ask me

every day about the money. What I do. She want buy a restaurant with the money. I not want restaurant. Much trouble. What I do.

I wish you come Thailand. I want see you. You are the wife of Henry I love him and I love you because you love him.

 Your friend.
 Arthit

Barbara was touched by this simple and quaint letter. She wrote back warning him that it might be two or three months before the legacy came through and she advised against the buying of a restaurant. Arthit hadn't yet answered.

3

It was May and there was an invigorating freshness in the air. Leonard set out one morning from his treasure-house of a flat in Rutland Gate on his habitual London walk to visit Wilson in his shop. Dapper in a grey suit, a light dark-grey overcoat and a grey trilby, Leonard strolled to Hyde Park Corner, negotiated the pedestrian tunnels and continued up Piccadilly and then turned into Berkeley Street passing the house (now offices) in which his maternal grandmother had once lived. He crossed Berkeley Square, entered Davies Street and soon reached Wilson's shop. Wilson was at his desk; his white head was visible through the shop's glass doors.

Leonard sat opposite his friend, who half rose and put out an arm inviting him to sit in the visitors' chair.

'I'm in love,' said Leonard.

'Oh dear, I thought you were past that nonsense.'

'I told you about him in a letter.'

'Mr Banana?'

'Yes. I called him that at first, but it's a bit condesending even if I don't use it to his face. He might not mind. The Thais like nicknames. His name is Amnuay.'

'What's that mean?'

'I don't know. It's a name. He telephoned me every day, usually at three o'clock in the afternoon when I was having my siesta. He woke me up. I never complained—'

'I'd never dare phone you at that hour. You *must* be in love.'

'D'you know what he said? He said he only liked old men – sixty, seventy, eighty OK, he said. He was seduced by an uncle when he was thirteen. He never wanted to marry, but was forced to by his parents. There are gays in his village but they are despised. In some villages, apparently they are accepted, even liked.'

'He'd better move to a tolerant village.'

'No, no, no,' said Leonard, crossly. 'Amnuay isn't openly gay. He lives with his wife and his son, aged sixteen, and he is a respected member of the community.'

Wilson emitted, 'Ha!'

Leonard continued. 'He's religious like most Thais, a believer anyway, Buddhist, of course. He told me he hoped we'd be reborn together. I'm afraid I was facetious. I said I'd like to be reincarnated as a water buffalo with him as a buffalo boy on my back. He was genuinely shocked.'

They both laughed.

'Have you a photograph?' asked Wilson.

Leonard produced from his wallet a postage-stamp size photo of Amnuay, full face, his nose broadened by his smile.

'Oh yes,' remarked Wilson. 'Not a beauty as you said in your letter, but he looks good-natured, sweet.'

'He is,' said Leonard emphatically. 'Come and have lunch, Wilson. We could go to my club, or that Italian place opposite Burlington Arcade. Your assistant is here, isn't she?'

'Beatrice? She's downstairs in the basement cataloguing a consignment of Japanese porcelain that's just arrived. Kutani. Modern.'

'Well, she could mind the shop, couldn't she?'

'I suppose so. I don't like to leave her alone for long these days.'

'You have alarms.'

'Yes, but no one would take any notice of them if they went off.'

'So come along then.'

'All right.' Wilson did not dislike the idea of lunching with Leonard, who, he well knew, would give him an excellent meal.

4

Yuichi, balancing a tray on the flat of his left hand, knocked on the door of Winifred's bedroom.

'Come in, dear,' cried the old lady.

'*Ohayo gozaimasu*, Wicku-san' was Yuichi's cheerful greeting.

'Dear boy.' Winifred pushed herself upon to her pillows and Yuichi placed on her lap the tray containing orange juice, tea, two slices of toast, butter and marmalade.

'This morning,' announced the young Japanese, 'you sit for me.'

'Oh, I don't think I'm up to sitting today. There's all that paraphernalia I have to put on.'

'You not sit for one week, Wicku-san. I mus' finish portrait.'

'All right then, Yuichi. You will help me dress, won't you?'

'Of course, Wicku-san. You call me when you ready.'

'Give me a kiss. You haven't given me my morning kiss.'

Yuichi kissed the old lady's flabby cheek.

'Thank you, dear. Now I feel better and perhaps up to sitting for you.'

5

'What about Trevor?' asked Wilson.

They had finished their Vitello Bocconcini and were waiting to be served with crème brûlée.

'You always ask me that,' replied Leonard, defensively. 'Well, what about him?'

'Have you given more thought to my suggestion? The one I made to you in Chiang Mai.'

'Of course it's entered my mind now and then, but I haven't come to any decision yet. After all, Wilson, as I keep pointing out, it was he who left me and he has a job. He's not destitute. I know you think I ought to buy him a flat, but if he wants a place he could get a mortgage, couldn't he?'

'It'd make such a difference to him if he had a place that was his and not to have the drain of paying monthly instalments for years.'

'I'll give it more thought, but flats are so expensive these days.'

'It needn't be in the West End or even in Kensington.'

'I should think not. Would a hundred thousand buy him a place? It's what I've left him in my will; he may as well have it now; it would mean a drop of about four thousand in my income.'

'You wouldn't notice that. A hundred and fifty would be better.'

'H'mm.' Leonard regarded the little round dish of crème brûlée that the waiter had just placed before him. 'I shouldn't have this, you know.'

6

Barbara handed Arthit's letter to Cecily, who had just arrived at Grasslands. Barbara had fetched her from Guildford Station.

'Don't you think it's touching?' asked Barbara.

'I'll tell you in a moment when I've read it.' Cecily took her reading glasses out of her handbag.

Barbara stood over the armchair in which Cecily was sitting, anxious to have her friend's reaction.

'Well, what do you think, Cecily?'

'I can't think why you write to him.' Cecily held out the letter, which Barbara took and then sat on the sofa by her friend's chair. They were in the drawing-room. It was a chilly afternoon although it was May; the central heating was on.

Barbara looked at the letter. 'I love his "flower is blooming" and "the tree is evergreen".'

'He must have used a dictionary,' said Cecily, deprecatingly. 'Are you going to reply?'

'Yes.'

'Why you keep up a correspondence with Henry's boyfriend is beyond my comprehension, Barbara.'

'It's strange, Cecily, but I feel attached to him, not in an amorous way, of course. He is a link with Henry, more than Neville is, or Jennifer even, because Henry loved him and he loved Henry.'

'How do you know? Surely he was just an outlet for Henry's homosexual tastes which developed, it seems, rather late in life. And Henry was the goose that laid the—'

Barbara bristled. 'No. Arthit isn't mercenary. Not at all. Why he says in his letter that he doesn't care about the legacy—'

'D'you believe that?'

'Yes I do. There was genuine love between them. I know, I'm absolutely certain that Arthit loved Henry. He told me so in a way that I'm sure was sincere.'

Cecily was silent for a moment, perhaps containing her scepticism and not wanting to hurt her friend, and then she asked, 'What are you going to advise about the legacy?'

'I'm going to advise against the restaurant idea.'

'Do you care, Barbara?'

'Yes, I do,' replied Barbara, defiantly.

'Why? Why do you care?'

'Because, because I'm interested in his welfare, his future. I'm going to advise him to put the money on deposit in the bank and use the interest to improve his standard of living and for the education of the children.' She had thought of suggesting to Arthit that he buy a sofa and get rid of the car seat, but she said nothing about that to Cecily, fearing her friend's sarcastic tongue.

'Didn't you say his wife was Chinese?' asked Cecily.

'She's a Chinese Thai.'

'Well, the Chinese are pretty shrewd with money, aren't they? I shouldn't worry about the legacy being wasted. A restaurant might be a good idea. Arthit won't have his salesman's job forever, will he?'

'I'm afraid that the wife will get hold of the money and use it as she likes. I don't mean she'd waste it necessarily, but Henry left the money to Arthit, not to his wife.'

'He must have known that Arthit was married. If a husband inherits a fortune – and presumably fifty thousand pounds is a large fortune to someone like Arthit – then you can't blame the wife for wanting to benefit from it too, even though it is in Thailand, where, I imagine, husbands hold the purse strings, or am I wrong?'

Barbara replied, 'I sensed that Arthit was a bit afraid of his wife, perhaps he felt guilty, and he let her make most of the decisions.'

'I see,' said Cecily, putting a finger to the side of her nose. 'So Arthit escaped from his wife's firm hand by having an affair with Henry. Henry was the father figure he could console himself with, and the consolation was well gilded, wasn't it?'

'I can't help being fascinated by Arthit and his affair with Henry. I don't know why I am, really.' Barbara rose. 'What will you have to drink, Cecily?'

'Are we going to have wine with supper?'

'Of course. The cellar is still fairly well stocked in spite of Neville's raids on it when he comes down.'

'A glass of white or red then, whatever we're having.'

'Both are equally easy.'

'White then, please.'

Later, during the evening meal which Barbara served in the kitchen at the rough old refectory table, Cecily, over the Stilton-cheese soup, asked, 'What news of Winifred and Yuichi?'

'Yuichi is still living with Winifred. I went down to Hove on Wednesday for lunch. Yuichi wasn't there. He was out at his art school.'

'You must have been disappointed, Barbara.'

Making no reply, Barbara collected the soup plates. 'Henry wouldn't have approved of our eating in the kitchen.'

'Did you eat in Winifred's kitchen.'

'Yes. A cold meal left by Yuichi. He evidently looks after her in a sort of way. Winifred seems content. She sings his praises. She does look frail, though, and so pallid. Her cheeks are like parchment. They have a cleaning woman at last and the flat looked in good shape. Winifred talked a lot about her neighbour who lives on the floor below and has a daughter in Tokyo, who has a young Japanese lover.'

'Oh dear, not another connection with the East,' said Cecily eyeing the roasted guinea fowl which Barbara had just brought out of the oven.

'I hope it's done enough,' said Barbara, looking at the bird doubtfully.

7

Trevor Hanson, unbeknown to both Wilson and to Leonard, had left his friend's flat near White City and gone to live with his parents in Norbury. He hated the suburban life at home, was utterly bored by his father and mother, and loathed commuting to Oxford Street every day. When he had lived with Leonard the store was just a short bus ride away, now he had to pile into a crowded train and at Victoria Station struggle on to a bus. He felt he couldn't sponge off his friend any longer. There was only one bedroom in Christopher's flat and Trevor had had to sleep on the sofa bed in the sitting-room, which meant he couldn't go to bed when he liked; also, although they were both gay and platonic friends, they found after three months they had had enough of each other. Having lived with Leonard for three years, Trevor had been satisfied with the society introduced to him by his older partner, most of them belonging to Leonard's generation, and he had no close friends of his own age except for Christopher. He had a number of gay acquaintances, some of whom worked in the store, but no bosom chums, no cosy confidants among them. He was lonely, even with Christopher. It was he who had suggested he left (Christopher was too kind a person to turn his friend out) and amicably they agreed to end the arrangement.

Soon after Trevor had moved to his parents' semi-detached villa in Norbury, a letter from a solicitor's office in Bedford Row came for him. His mother was nosy. 'It looks official. It's from a law firm,' she said. 'I hope you haven't been getting into trouble.' The letter was marked: PLEASE FORWARD, but this wasn't necessary since Trevor had left Christopher's.

Trevor, more anxious than his mother to know the contents of the letter, managed to contain his curiosity, ardent though it was. He took it to his office and opened it when his boss and the other assistant in the Display Section were out of the room.

The letter requested him to furnish the solicitor with his account number and the address of his bank so that the sum of one hundred thousand pounds could be paid into it. The donor wished to remain anonymous. Trevor trembled and blushed; his body tingled. He had often dreamed of winning a million pounds or so in the Lottery and like half the population or more in Britain he fantasised over the spending of it. First, he'd resign from the store, then he'd acquire an apartment like Leonard's – perhaps Leonard would sell him his; he would go on a world tour and buy a Mercedes or a Jaguar, or both, not a Rolls or a Bentley, too ostentatious and they get scratched by envious louts. He'd have to tell his parents; he'd give them one hundred thousand pounds; but that was what he'd been given now: one hundred thousand pounds, not several million; he'd not give his parents anything; he'd not tell them about it; better not; they would want to know where it came from, and if they knew they would tell him to give it back. It had come from Leonard, of course. Should he thank him? Fancy having a hundred thousand pounds to spare! Leonard must have more millions than he realised. In the lunch hour he decided to call on Wilson Gill in Davies Street. Wilson was behind his desk in the shop.

'Oh, hello,' Wilson said, cautiously. 'You've just missed Leonard. He's gone to his club to lunch with someone. Sit down, Trevor.'

Trevor sat gingerly on the chair opposite Wilson. 'I've just 'ad this from a lawyer.' He handed the letter across the desk to Wilson, who read it carefully. 'It comes from Leonard, doesn't it? Did you know about it?'

Wilson, being a compassionate and a modest man did not tell Trevor he had been persuading Leonard for months to give Trevor a decent sum, and instead merely said, 'Yes.'

'Why did Leonard pay me off now and not before, if he meant to?'

'He's been thinking about it ever since you left him.'

'I didn't expect to be paid off. In a way it's insultin'.'

'It would be silly to take it like that.'

'It's the sort of treatment a dismissed mistress gets.'

'Better than a slap in the face with a wet fish,' said Wilson, forcing a laugh.

'I'll give it back,' said Trevor, who had no intention of doing so.

'That would be foolish. It's meant to help you to buy a flat; that was Leonard's idea. Now, you must excuse me; I have a luncheon appointment.'

Trevor quickly rose and said resentfully, 'Sorry to have troubled you.'

'No trouble at all. I wouldn't contact Leonard if I were you, but write a letter of acknowledgement to the lawyer when you get the money. Let me know how you get on.'

'You mean let you know 'ow I spent the money so you can tell Leonard.'

'No I didn't mean that at all' – although of course he did.

8

Winifred gave a deep sigh as she sat in the chair in her regalia: a long Thai silk dress, striped in yellow, black and magenta, a Spanish fan decorated with red roses in her right hand, an auburn shawl draped round her shoulders, and the auburn wig which hid her grey hair. 'Let it be a short sitting today, Yuichi, I'm tired.'

'I wan' do again your hand, the left one; prease show your fingers; don't hide them in your hand li' a boxer.'

Winifred laughed. She loved his quaint phraseology. 'You mean not to make a fist.' She stretched out the fingers of her left hand which remained on her lap. 'Must I also hold up the fan?'

'Prease, Wicku-san.'

Yuichi busied himself with his palette and brushes, concentrating on the hand he was painting. After a while, the fan fell out of the old lady's right hand; her left one did not move. Yuichi looked at Winifred. Her head had slumped forward, her chin on her chest. Yuichi continued to work on her left hand for some minutes. He then looked at her again. 'Wicku-san!' he cried. No answer. 'You asleep? OK. Your left hand is all right. I go on painting.' He mixed some more paint and applied it to the canvas. 'There,' he said, 'that better. Wicku-san, I finished.' There was no reply. 'Wicku-san!' Yuichi moved across to Winifred's chair. 'Wicku-san!' he cried again. He put a finger under the old lady's chin and gently raised her head and then let go; the head lolled down again. 'Wicku-san!' Yuichi shouted. He raised her head again; the eyes were half shut and glazed. 'Wicku-san!' He felt her pulse and finding no throb he put an ear against her heart. 'Wicku-san!' He realised she was dead. He did not panic, being oriental, death was less of a shock to him than it would have been to a Westerner; to him death was distressing, but more to him than to Winifred. What should he do? He must get help. He thought for a moment, then went to the telephone. He'd ring Barbara, Winifred's niece. What was her number? He didn't know it. He left the flat and ran down the stairs and rang Gertrude's bell urgently. Gertrude opened her door.

'What on earth's the matter?' she asked, crossly.

Yuichi said, 'Wicku-san, Mrs Chadwick, she dead just now.'

'What?'

'I paint her and she die.'

'Are you serious, Yuichi?'

'Prease help. What I do?'

'I'll come up. We'll call Ron, the caretaker.'

9

'Darling, Winifred is dead,' Veronica said to Neville as soon as he had come in from the City.

'Winifred?'

'Your great aunt,' Veronica said impatiently. 'Barbara rang just now to tell us. You haven't forgotten her, have you?'

'I never called her Winifred. She was always Aunt Winnie to me. So ancient Aunt Winnie is no more. I wonder how much she left.'

'You would think of the money.'

'I do work for a bank and isn't that what most people think of first when a relation dies?'

'Aren't you sorry?'

'Yes, of course,' replied Neville, not sounding the least distressed. 'Of course I am. I knew her all my life. Hadn't seen her since last Christmas at Grasslands when that awful shop assistant and that Jap were there. I hope she hasn't left her money to the Jap. He was still living with her, wasn't her?'

'Yes. Will you go to the funeral?'

'I must. Mother would want me to. You ought to go too.'

'My going will have to depend on my work and on the baby. I'll have to see.'

'Try to come, darling. Mother would like it.'

10

Gertrude got Barbara's number from Enquiries and as soon as Yuichi had rung Grasslands with the news of Winifred's demise, Barbara set off for Hove in her late husband's Mercedes. She was relieved to find that Yuichi was quite composed and sensible. To be alone in a foreign land with a dead old lady on one's hands would have been a nasty predicament for many, but not such a bad one for Yuichi, apparently.

Gertrude had contacted the caretaker, who had called the police and Winifred's doctor. A fatal heart attack was diagnosed. The body was placed in the striped Thai silk dress on the bed in the spare room, where Yuichi had been painting her. An undertaker was contacted and the remains were to be removed the next day to his funeral parlour.

After the arrangements had been made and Barbara and Yuichi were alone in Winifred's flat, Yuichi expressed surprise over the fact that a wake by the corpse was not to be held that night with relatives and friends attending. 'We don't do that in England,' Barbara explained. 'They do in Ireland, I believe.'

'In Japan we sit by the body all night. A priest he say prayers. Next day we burn.'

'We're not as quick as that in England.'

11

Barbara got in touch with Winifred's lawyer, who informed her that there was a copy of the Will in the flat. She guessed it was in the bureau in Winifred's bedroom. Yuichi knew where the key of the bureau was hidden – 'She show me one day; she put it in that vase' and the main drawer was soon opened and the Will found. Barbara was the residuary legatee and there were generous legacies to relations and friends. Neville and Jennifer were left one hundred thousand pounds each, and a recent codicil instructed that Yuichi was to receive twenty five thousand. When Barbara informed Neville of the news (she knew he longed to know how much he had been left), he had been pleased and relieved that all the old lady's fortune had not gone to the Japanese.

'How much did Aunt Winnie have?'

'I don't know, dear. I shall have to ask the lawyer tomorrow. I'm glad Yuichi's been left something. He's been so good. In the codicil it says: "To my friend Yuichi Matsumoto with gratitude for his devoted attention. I hope this sum will help him complete his studies". The portrait is left to me. You don't want it, do you?'

'God no!'

Barbara was surprised at the number of fellow mourners who attended Winifred's service in Hove Parish Church, at which Winifred had only worshipped on feast days. She hadn't realised that Winifred had known so many people. Only she, Yuichi, Gertrude, Neville, Veronica, Cecily and Ron went to the Committal at the Crematorium. Her ashes, according to Winifred's wishes, were to be put in her husband's tomb in the graveyard of the church at Hartfield, Sussex, where Winifred had lived in a large Tudor-style house in spacious grounds until she was widowed.

Yuichi had behaved perfectly and been an inestimable help. Barbara had to call on her reserves of self-control to prevent herself from trying to seduce him again. He gave her no provocative sign as he had on that day when she visited Winifred some months ago. Living in such close proximity with Yuichi in the flat was disturbing. When she asked him his plans, he was vague. He seemed to have none and didn't know where he would go. He had a student visa and could stay in

England provided he attended some college. Barbara felt sorry for him. Suddenly, at breakfast on the morning after the funeral, she, who was returning to Grasslands that day, invited Yuichi to stay with her until he found more suitable accommodation. She knew she asked him, not so much because she was sorry for him, but because she longed to repeat the experience she had had in Jennifer's flat; it had been no more than a half-undressed romp on the sofa, but thrilling nevertheless.

Barbara had given the invitation on the spur of the moment, her voice shaking. Yuichi had replied, 'Yes, I like very much. My art school in Brighton, what I do?'

'You could change to one in Guildford, I'm sure. Can you drive?'

'Yes. Japanese licence OK in England if I have international and I get before I come to England. I think that perhaps I may drive a car. In Japan we drive on left side so easy for me.'

'You can drive us to Grasslands when you've packed your things. What about the portrait?'

'I take. I can finish at Grasslands.'

'I shall have to be coming down here a lot to sort things out, but I think it better for you not to be alone here and you would like to come to Grasslands, wouldn't you?'

'Oh yes, Mrs Rane. I li' very much. You very kind.'

'I think we'd get on, don't you, Yuichi?' She gave him a look raising her eyebrow.

'Get on?' he inquired, seeming puzzled.

'I mean, you and I would agree.' She raised her eyebrows again and gave him another look.

'Agree?' Again his face showed incomprehension.

'I mean,' said Barbara, flustered, 'you would not mind being alone with me at Grasslands, which, as you know, is not very near a town.'

'Of course,' Yuichi answered.

'Good.' Barbara took this to mean that he wouldn't mind being alone with her. From previous conversations with him she had learnt that the Japanese were uncertain about the correct response to a negative question, and that his 'Of course' should be understood as 'Of course not.'

12

One morning a week or so later Leonard paid one of his customary visits to Wilson in his shop.

'You heard the news, I suppose,' said Wilson.

'What news?'

'Winifred Chadwick died. Didn't you see the notice in *The Times*?'

'I always forget to read the Deaths column. Who is she anyway? Did I know her?'

'She was Barbara Lane's aunt, Jennifer's great aunt, and Yuichi's, er, mother-figure, you might say.'

'I remember now,' said Leonard, his interest aroused. 'Tell me more. What will Yuichi do? Who will be his next surrogate parent, or keeper?'

'He's gone to live with Barbara Lane at her house near Guildford.'

'He has, has he?'

'He had a roll with Barbara once?'

'How do you know all this?' asked Leonard.

'I told you in a letter when you were in Chiang Mai last winter, before I came out to join you. Trevor told me and Veronica at dinner. Yuichi told Trevor.'

'Who is Veronica?'

'You do forget people, Leonard. Veronica is Neville's wife, Barbara's daughter-in-law. I often dine with them. They live in Kensington.'

'You have so many acquaintances. I can't keep up with them. Tell me more about Yuichi.'

'But you're in love, Leonard. You said so the other day. You can't be interested in Yuichi now.'

'He was so marvellous in bed, and my Thai lover, Amnuay, is so far away. I need solace.'

'Barbara has put her house up for sale, but has not had any offers yet. Why don't you go down to Guildford on the pretext of looking at the house as a prospective purchaser?'

'I could call on her as a friend. Not only did I meet her in Chiang Mai, I entertained her there, more than once. Have you the address?'

'Yes.'

13

'Very beautiful,' said Yuichi to Barbara when they entered the gates of Grasslands and continued up the drive to the substantial Edwardian red brick house. Yuichi was at the wheel. He had driven very much to Barbara's satisfaction. The daffodils and the tulips were over, but the stocks and the wallflowers were making a good show and on either side of the front door were beds of peonies, most of them in bud. These excited Yuichi, who on getting out of the car went up to them.

'*Botan*,' he cried. 'these we call *botan* in Japanese. We have in Japan and many painters they paint *botan*.'

'My husband, Henry, was very fond of peonies, but they attract ants. Of course when you were here over Christmas nothing was out.' Barbara fumbled in her bag for the keys of the house. Yuichi unloaded the boot and the back of the car and carried his belongings and Barbara's suitcases into the hall.

'I'm going to put you in Henry's room.' She did not add that it had a communicating door with hers. 'And you can use the study as a studio.'

'You are very kind.'

It was nearly eight o'clock; they had not left Hove until after six; but since it was June it was not yet dark. 'Let's go into the kitchen and see what we can find in the fridge. Can you cook, Yuichi?'

The Japanese smiled. 'I cook a little for Wicku-san. Not good.'

'And let's have a drink. We can unpack after supper.'

Barbara opened a bottle of claret. 'You don't drink, do you, Yuichi?'

'I start when I was with Wicku-san. She teach me. I do not like before. Now I like.'

Barbara laughed. 'What a wicked old thing Wicku-san was!'

'What you say?'

'Nothing. I'm glad you drink. It's more companionable if you like a glass or two of wine.' She took two glasses out of a cupboard, filled them with wine and handed Yuichi one of then. 'I hope you'll be happy here,' she said, raising her glass, which shook a little.

'You very kind.'

Barbara busied herself preparing a ham omelette and a salad, which they ate in the kitchen at the refectory table. 'Henry would never eat in here,' she said. 'He insisted on having all meals in the dining-room, even breakfast; and I have no staff. The gardener's wife comes in to clean and tidy in the mornings from Monday to Friday. I do the cooking and the shopping. Cecily comes down often for weekends. You know her, don't you?'

'I meet her at the apartment of Mr Neville and Mrs Veronica.'

'Of course you did. They were here at Christmas when you came down, and I remember that dinner-party when Jennifer brought you to the flat in Kensington, and we had a joke about swordfish. D'you remember?'

'Yes, I do.'

'I can't remember what swordfish is in Japanese but you told us.'

'*Kajiki maguro.*'

'Yes, but you can't expect me to remember that.'

Barbara chattered on about her family, her house, how she

was trying to sell it, the problem of where to live when she did; should it be in London? She couldn't live isolated in the country by herself, could she. The house was too big, wasn't it? Neville didn't want it. She wondered why he didn't now he had a son and Veronica liked Grasslands and surely it was better for them to live outside London; many people commuted from Guildford. Henry had for years. On went her nervous flow. Yuichi, only half understanding, listened patiently to it. At last she said, 'I'm talking too much. Let me show you your room.'

They went upstairs. In Henry's room, Barbara indicated the communicating door. 'I'll leave it unlocked,' she said pointedly, 'in case you need something. Have a shower or a bath, if you like. The water should be hot. I think I'll go to bed. I'm tired. These last few days have been exhausting. Goodnight, Yuichi. I'm so glad you're here.' She held out her hand, which trembled when he took it.

'Goodni', Mrs Rane.'

'Not Mrs Lane, or Rane, please. Barbara.'

'Goodni' Barbarla. Barbarla difficult. I call you, Barbu-san.'

She chuckled nervously. 'I like that. Goodnight again, Yuichi.' She left him hoping that the goodnights were not final.

She went to bed and lay there, her heart pounding. She could hear him moving about his room, unpacking, she supposed, and having a shower. And then without a knock, Yuichi, wearing only his underpants, entered Barbara's room through the communicating door. Her bedside light was still on. She threw back the bedclothes and he got into the bed beside her.

'You want, isn't it?'

She answered by pulling him towards her and, shaking with desire covered his smooth, hairless body with passionate kisses. He responded with ardour. She groaned with delight. As he ejaculated he shouted, '*Iku, iku, iku!*'

The shouts of the esoteric word increased the excitement of the moment.

14

The following few days passed pleasantly. Yuichi was helpful. He drove her to a supermarket, assisted the gardener's wife with some of the household chores and spent part of each night in Barbara's bed. She had never had such a wonderful lovemaking. Compared with Henry, Yuichi was like magic. She put off Cecily, who wanted to come down for the weekend. The two spent one hectic night after another.

Yuichi fixed up his easel in the study downstairs and started to put final touches to the portrait of Winifred.

One morning Barbara interrupted him. 'Leonard Crampstead is on the phone. He wants to come down to see the house. You knew him, didn't you?'

'Yes,' answered Yuichi, preoccupied, appraising the painting.

'He wants to come tomorrow. I'll ask him to lunch, shall I?'

'OK,' murmured Yuichi, absorbed in the portrait. He was wearing his blue and white *yukata*, a cotton bath robe with wide sleeves and kept together by an *obi*, a long black sash. Barbara liked to see him in this garment, which made him look more Japanese, more exotic.

15

Leonard arrived in a hired car with a driver.

'It's good of you to let me come,' he said to Barbara, graciously as she welcomed him on the doorstep.

'It's good to see you again,' she replied.

'What a splendid garden you have! It seems to be at the peak of its glory!'

'Do come in, Leonard.'

'I'll send the driver off to have lunch. He can come back for me. What time shall I say? Two-thirty?'

'Yes, I should think so.'

Leonard spoke to the driver and followed Barbara into the house; she led him into the drawing-room.

'Is Yuichi here?' he asked, unable to hide his eagerness.

'He's gone up to change. He's been painting my late aunt's portrait. Do sit down. A drink? I've put some sherry out, but if you'd rather have gin and tonic or a Campari and soda or something I can get it.'

Leonard sat in an armchair. 'Sherry would be fine,' he said, eyeing the decanter which stood with three glasses on a silver tray placed on a small round mahogany table near a china cabinet.

Barbara filled the three glasses, gave one to Leonard and took one for herself. She had taken trouble with her appearance, carefully making up her face and prinking her dyed fair hair; she was wearing a dark-blue, calf-length dress; a string of pearls adorned her neck where the skin was loose. She hoped she didn't look more than her fifty years and that there were no signs of the previous night's rampage.

Leonard wore a pink shirt with a green, yellow and red flowery tie, a Thai tie, a light brown suit and brown suede shoes.

'I didn't realise that the house was so big, so elegant,' Leonard said. 'How much land is there?'

'Ten acres. They include a copse and two fields. We used to have ponies for the children. The fields can be let or sold should the new owner wish to do so. Are you thinking of leaving London?'

'I'm tired of London,' lied Leonard. 'I've been contemplating a move to the country for some years. This place seems ideal.'

Yuichi appeared, wearing his yellow, polo-neck pullover and jeans. Leonard rose. Yuichi bowed and then shook hands with him. Leonard's eyes sparkled and looked into his.

'I've poured out a glass of sherry for you, Yuichi,' said the hostess, who had noticed the look Leonard had given the young man, but she hid her displeasure.

Perfectly composed, Yuichi took his glass from the silver tray, held it up and said, 'Good ruck,' regarding Leonard, who sniggered and then coughed to hide his amusement, and regained his chair. Yuichi sat on the sofa between the two armchairs; he held himself stiffly and looked at the Persian rug in front of the fireplace.

After a silence, Leonard remarked, 'This is a delightful house. I can't understand why you want to sell it.'

'Too big. It's impossible for me to live here alone,' explained Barbara. 'Neville doesn't want it, nor does Jennifer. You saw a lot of Jennifer in Chiang Mai, I understand. She doesn't write often. In one of her rare letters she mentioned you.'

Yuichi continued to stare at the carpet.

'She moved into one of the houses owned by the Golden Plaza Hotel,' said Leonard.

'She told me. Is she happy, d'you think?' asked Barbara.

'Yes, I should say she was. The heat was bothering her a bit. It was over a hundred when I left, but it cools down at night considerably.'

'How awful, though, a hundred!'

'When the rains come the temperature drops to a certain extent, not all that much, though.'

Yuichi rose. He had finished his sherry. Barbara looked at him questioningly. 'I go to kitchen to see if food all right.'

'No need. The smoked salmon is on the dining-room table and the pilaff will keep warm in the rice cooker. Oh, there's the salad—' She rose.

'I do,' offered Yuichi.

'No, no, you talk to Leonard.' She left the room.

Yuichi, in the manner of the master of the house, stood with his back to the fireplace. 'You like more sherry, Renardo-san?'

Leonard smiled at Yuichi's version of his name which the young man had used previously on intimate occasions. 'Please,' he said. When Yuichi had replenished the glasses, Leonard asked 'What are your plans?'

'I want to finish Wicku-san's portrait, and then I must join art school. Barbu-san she say I can go to art school in Guildford.'

'It would be much better if you went back to that college you were at in London before you went to live in Hove.' Leonard sipped his drink and through his thick glasses looked hard at Yuichi, who again stood with his back to the fireplace. 'You could stay in my flat.'

'You very kind, Renardo-san.'

Leonard rose and approached Yuichi. He put his left hand on the young man's shoulder and gave him a quick kiss on the cheek. 'Come and see me in London,' he whispered. 'You know where I am. London would be much better than here.'

Yuichi accepted the kiss and the invitation passively; his pale face remained solemn.

'You will, won't you?' pleaded Leonard.

'Ready!' Barbara's cry came from the long passage that led to the kitchen. 'Ready!'

Yuichi moved away from Leonard. 'We mus' go,' he said and led his former patron and lover to the dining-room, where Barbara awaited them.

Throughout the meal, Leonard, apart from when he was exchanging remarks with his hostess, stared at Yuichi. Barbara noticed and wondered. She knew, of course, about Leonard's tastes, but she was unaware that he had enticed Yuichi into his bed even after the young man had gone to live with Jennifer in her London flat. Barbara was jealous when, after the meal, she followed Yuichi and Leonard in the study and heard flattering praise of the portrait. Leonard again expressed his enchantment with the house and hinted that he might be a prospective buyer. They toured the house. More than once when they were visiting a room Barbara saw the hairy back of Leonard's hand touch the back of Yuichi's. Inwardly, she seethed. When they returned to the drawing-room, Leonard, after asking permission, lit a cigar.

Barbara looked out of the window. 'Your car is here,' she said.

Leonard rose, cigar in hand. He thanked Barbara profusely for her hospitality, and in the hall firmly bid her goodbye. 'Don't bother to see me off,' he said. Yuichi followed him out to the car.

'You have Japanese car,' Yuichi remarked.

'Is it Japanese? I hadn't noticed. It's hired. I can't drive and don't have a car. I hire one when I need one. Much cheaper. No worries.'

In spite of Leonard's order Barbara appeared at the front door. Through the open back window of the car, Leonard said to Yuichi, 'Don't forget. Ring me up. Let's meet soon. Your painting is excellent. It shows great talent. I'll speak to Wilson about it. I think it ought to be put in for the Summer Exhibition at the Royal Academy next year.'

'*Sayonara.*' Yuichi, bowing, stepped back and the car moved off.

'Goodbye,' cried Barbara.

Leonard waved his cigar at the two who were now standing side by side.

'He likes you,' said Barbara.

'Yes, he like me.'

'Do you like him?'

'He very kind.'

Barbara wished, not for the first time, that Yuichi would give a direct answer.

Part Six

1

In August Sylvia met Toshi in Kyoto, a sauna-bath of a place in the summer, but easy for Sylvia to reach from Tokyo and Toshi from Saga. Toshi arrived first from Osaka, having flown there from Fukuoka in Kyushu and then taken a train to Kyoto.

He was on the platform when the sleek, blue and white express silently drew in to Kyoto Station. Sylvia had told him the number of her carriage and he knew exactly where to stand.

When Sylvia alighted, there he was. 'Oh Toshi, how wonderful!' she cried, dropping her suitcase and giving him a hug and a warm kiss on the mouth. Her display of affection embarrassed him; she knew it would, but she couldn't resist it. Toshi bent down and took her suitcase. 'It has wheels,' she said. 'You can wheel it.'

'It not heavy,' Toshi replied. 'I carry. Better.'

Along with the troops of arriving passengers they edged their way to the concrete steps that led down to the exit.

'I check in at hotel. It near Kawaramachi, main street, in centre of town,' said Toshi as they were descending the steep flights to ground level.

'You *are* good, Toshi. Oh I am so pleased to see you, darling. I missed you terribly.'

'I miss you, too.'

'Did you really?'

They queued for a taxi.

'God, it's hot!' said Sylvia.

'Kyoto very hot in summer,' replied Toshi. 'It call steaming rice bowl.'

In the taxi, Sylvia asked, 'Have you been here before?'

'Only when I was school student. All schools in Japan they make trip to Kyoto.'

'What ugly buildings!' They had reached the middle of Kawaramachi where department stores, pachinko parlours, restaurants and cafés abound. 'It's just like anywhere else,' she complained. They turned into Oike-dori and were soon outside their hotel, a tall but narrow building. Sylvia went up to the front desk – called *fronto* in Japanese – and was told that she needn't register as Toshi had already done so. The face of the young clerk in black coat and tie gave her no appraising sign as his counterpart probably would have done in the West. The bedroom was as small as a cell but efficiently air-cooled. There was only just enough room for the twin beds, which Sylvia was pleased to notice were close together, a little desk, a television set and one upright chair; the bathroom was equipped with all the necessary appliances but there was hardly space enough to turn round in it.

The advantage of the hot summer months in Japan is that everyone wears few clothes. Sylvia wore a cotton dress with short sleeves and Toshi a sports shirt and jeans. Soon their bodies were free of this skimpy apparel and they were in each other's arms.

'I love you,' said Sylvia, momentarily breaking away from her lover's embrace. 'Have you found a girlfriend in Saga?'

'I not. You find new boy in Tokyo?'

'No.' This was true. Sylvia had not once seen the persistent local greengrocer.

Sylvia and Toshi had an enjoyable and harmonious time both in the bedroom and visiting temples. She wanted to see the Golden Pavilion (because of Mishima's novel) and Ryoanji, as the stone garden was so famous, so many people had written about it, including Sacheverell Sitwell, who had described it twice: once before seeing it and once after, and he said, Sylvia was amused to remember, that his first description was better than his second. She told Toshi about this and he said 'I see', but she didn't think he did. He was not unwilling to accompany her on these tourists excursions; it's hard for a Japanese to visit Kyoto without paying homage to at least one renowned temple or shrine.

The three days passed happily. Their parting at Kyoto Station was painful. Sylvia left first. Toshi saw her off and waited until the great express slowly moved away; he ran along the platform for a short distance waving. Sylvia was distraught. He seemed truly to love her. Did he really? It was damnable his being as far away as Saga. She recalled as the train sped past the lake at Hamamatsu, where Toshi was born and where his parents lived, that he had behaved in a less boyish way than before. He had made decisions and taken her in charge. She liked this new Toshi. Somehow the few months in Saga had caused him to grow up, perhaps because he was on his own and no longer under the protection of herself or his other middle-aged mother figure. The worrying thing was that now he had become a man would he no longer want her? But his tender attention in Kyoto persuaded her that he really did care for her.

2

August in Chiang Mai is cooler than that month in Tokyo or Kyoto. The rains have begun in Thailand; heavy showers bring down the temperature; they also turned the lane in which Jennifer lived into a quagmire. It didn't matter getting wet, even wet through; saturated clothes soon dried. But the mud was a nuisance and the *tuk-tuk* men didn't like driving through it.

The holiday with Somsak at Krabi on the Andaman Sea had passed off without any ructions; besides, Somsak was too passive a character to have a confrontation with anyone; he would probably run away from a crisis. Jennifer only surmised that this was so, since he always agreed with her suggestions. 'Shall we swim?' she would say when they were both lolling on sun-beds under the palms outside their cabin.

'*Lao ta khun* – up to you,' he would reply with a smile.

Somsak, though, didn't do very much lolling. He often left Jennifer to lounge about by herself with a book and went off with his sketch pad to draw: trees, the sea, fishing boats, and he did several portraits of her. Jennifer, who knew something about art (she had studied art history at Sussex University) was impressed by his draughtsmanship, which was well above the standard of the average school teacher of art in Thailand.

Somsak was no conversationalist. At meals in the hotel restaurant, when lying on the beach or in bed, he never said anything. Once she asked him what he was thinking about. 'I think about my art,' he replied.

Not being certain of his situation and having longed to know about it ever since she had met him, one night when they were lying in bed together she asked him if he were married, though she had assumed he couldn't be judging by the bare shack he inhabited behind his school, but in Thailand one couldn't be sure.

'No,' he replied, quite unsurprised by the question. 'Many people ask me. I say, "I married to my art."'

She didn't know whether to laugh at this answer or not. She simply said, 'I see.'

'My father, mother, they push me to marry. I do not want.'

'Oh, really?' Jennifer had thought of marrying him herself. She had grown fond of him. He was a simple person, in need, she felt, of encouragement, of a supporter, of someone who had confidence in him, in his art. During the holiday in Krabi, her feelings had changed. She had grown to love him more. He wasn't much good in bed, but he was handsome, gentle, and, in his way, fond of her, she felt. Sex, she began to realise, wasn't all that important. She now understood that he didn't care whether he fucked her or not. When she asked him to with hints and signs, he submitted to her desire, out of politeness, she guessed. He still came too quickly, and after he had come he lost interest in her body. He wasn't very sexy, she decided, unlike many Thais. She was prepared to accept this because she wanted to be with him. She enjoyed his quiet presence. She made up her mind to try to help him.

'Somsak,' she said one morning. 'Your drawing is good. Why don't you try colour?'

'I cannot see colour,' he explained. 'I cannot get colour right.'

'You must start with watercolours. I'll get a box sent from England. I'll advise you. I have faith in you. I believe you could become a real artist, Somsak.'

'That is my dream.'

3

August in London can be hot, but never as hot as it is in Kyoto, Tokyo or in Chiang Mai.

Matthew and Jun had settled into their service flat in Gorden Mansions, just off Sloane Street. They were to stay three weeks, the longest time Jun had ever spent outside Japan. Jun, on holiday from school, liberated from the chains of matrimony, was excited to be abroad, away from the restrictions of Japan; it is natural to feel freer when one is a foreigner than when in one's own country, having to belong, having to conform. Jun had told Matthew that he didn't want to be with him all the time, that he wanted to go off on his own, that he had several Japanese friends who lived in London whom he wanted to see.

'Where do you want to go?'

'I want to see my friends and I want to look around,' replied Jun. 'I want to learn to manage in a foreign city by myself.'

'I have to go and see my sister on Friday, so you can have

three days to yourself. She has asked me to stay till Monday. I'd better, I suppose. I didn't see her last summer when we were here.'

'I know. You were jealous of Colin Sibley. You thought I wanted to have a secret meeting with him. You wouldn't let me out of your eyes.'

'Sight,' corrected Matthew, pedagogically. 'In any case Mark, Sylvia's son and Colin's lover, wouldn't have liked your flirting with Colin. As it happens you can't see him. He's in New York with Mark. I forget what play they're doing. Where will you go, Jun?'

'Just somewhere.' Jun smiled. He knew how to tease Matthew. Since Jun had left his wife and returned to Matthew's embrace, the two had lived in harmony; however, his brief married life had acted as a sort of trial-by-fire out of which he had come more adult, less dependent. Like many gay couples they were beginning to arrive at a tacit understanding: infidelity was permissible, provided it was a passing passion. The affection between them remained firm even if it was temporarily bent. Marriage, an experience which Matthew had never known, had given Jun a different status. He could now say he had been married, while Matthew was still a bachelor, and in Japan it was more acceptable for a man to be divorced than to have never had a wife.

4

Matthew's sister, Mary, was unmarried. She was sixty, five years older than Matthew, and had spent her working life teaching history at a select school for girls in Sussex. She had taken early retirement and had bought with some of her inheritance – on her mother's death she had been left two thirds of the estate, while Matthew had only got a third, but an aunt had left him a decent sum – a cottage at Chiddingfold in Surrey. She was on the parish and diocesan councils, several committees of charitable organisations, and had cronies in for tea and bridge. When Matthew was asked if he had any relations he would mention his sister. 'A good woman,' he would say, 'too good for me.' He would not add that her getting the bulk of the family estate still rankled. He presumed she knew he was gay (perhaps their mother had known and therefore had adjusted her will), although the subject was never touched on. He wondered if she were lesbian since she had remained single.

He took the train to Guildford, where she met him with her little car.

'I'm glad you have a Japanese motor,' remarked Matthew.

'I didn't buy it out of loyalty to you,' she laughed. 'I got it because it's well designed and efficiently made. How is Japan? Are you going to stay there forever?'

Matthew sighed when he entered his poky bedroom with low beams, and he did not like sharing a bathroom with his sister. She produced a shepherd's pie for supper – Mary wasn't interested in food and therefore wasn't much of a cook; at least she liked wine and the Bulgarian red was quite drinkable.

'I only have cheese to follow,' Mary warned Matthew. 'I never have "sweets" as people call "puddings" today, and as for "starters" – vulgar word – they're out as far as I'm concerned. I hope you don't mind. There is some fruit.'

'The less I eat the better.'

'You've put on weight, Matthew.'

'I know.'

'By the way, tomorrow morning I've arranged to visit a house. The owner, a Mrs Lane, is expecting us. She will show us round. The agent is busy and she has agreed to this. I'm pleased. I don't like looking at places with agents. One has to listen to their claptrap.'

'Are you thinking of moving, then, Mary?'

'Heavens no! I just want to satisfy my curiosity. Outside a village called Dunfold is a house with the name of Grasslands. It's up for sale. I hear that the owner was killed in a car crash in

Thailand and his widow, Mrs Lane, wants to sell the place. I saw an advertisement in the local paper, rang the agent and fixed an appointment to view the house tomorrow at eleven. I've often driven past the entrance to the property. You can see a bungalow by the gates but you can't see the house from the road: the drive winds, there are trees. You will come with me, won't you Matthew?'

'Of course.'

'And you will pretend you are interested in purchasing the place?'

'Yes, my dear, if that is what you desire. It's unlike you to view a place you do not wish to buy.'

'I told the agent that my brother was coming back from the East and was looking for a property in the district.'

'Oh, did you? You make me sound like a tycoon, a nineteenth-century nabob.'

'The place has intrigued me ever since I came to live here.'

'Why?'

'I've just longed to see behind those trees. It's simply curiosity.'

5

When Jun had separated from his wife, he renewed his friendship with his buddies in Mr Lady, the gay bar he had frequented before his marriage. Matthew had condoned Jun's visits to the bar, where foreigners were not really welcome, although out of jealousy he had not approved in spite of his own lapses in fidelity.

Some of the customers of Mr Lady liked to go to a room at the back of the premises to have their faces made up. One of the barmen, who during the day worked for a cosmetics firm, was an artist at rejuvenating, albeit temporarily, old features. A tired businessman would, on his way home to his wife, drop by Mr Lady and submit to the expert applying of maquillage by the barman whose name was Shinichi; in the bar he was known as 'Shuko', and he wore drag. The businessman, after receiving the 'treatment' would sit at the bar admiring his reflection in the mirror. For an hour or so he would revel in an atmosphere much different from the office whence he had come or from the home whither he was going. This brief respite from convention acted like a restorative and proved more efficacious than one of those little bottles of vitamins on sale in pharmacies, and he left the bar to catch his commuter train refreshed.

In Mr Lady Jun met one of his cronies who had recently returned from a holiday in Europe. The friend told Jun of a bar off Oxford Street, which he assured him was 'very interesting', using the English words with emphasis. Jun took advantage of Matthew's absence for the weekend and went to the bar. It was packed. The bar upstairs was hedged with drinkers whose eyes swivelled to inspect new arrivals. As instructed by his friend, Jun went downstairs and found himself amongst a cluster of Orientals: Chinese, Thai and Japanese. For Jun it was easy to detect the last, of whom there were only three. He soon fell into conversation (it was a relief to speak his own language) with a fellow countryman who told him he was a painter and had been in England for nearly a year. He recounted his experiences with Leonard, Jennifer, Trevor, Winifred Chadwick and Barbara Lane, explaining that he preferred mature people and was indifferent to their sex. Jun mentioned Matthew and his broken marriage and said that he didn't care for women at all. Yuichi understood this and said that he was living with Barbara at Grasslands and fucked her in order to please her and in return for free board and lodging. He had come to London to spend the weekend with Leonard, who had a dinner engagement that evening. The two Japanese got on well and Yuichi suggested that he came back to Leonard's flat for the night. 'He not mind,' said Yuichi. Jun was much struck by Yuichi's suave and sophisticated manner and accepted the invitation.

6

'So you live in Japan, Mr er—'

'Bennet.' For the second time Matthew supplied Barbara with his surname. 'Yes, in Tokyo.'

'I have a young Japanese artist staying with me, but he's not here at the moment; he's gone to London for the weekend. He's called Yuichi – there, I've forgotten his other name.'

'It's Matsumoto,' Cecily, who was spending the weekend at Grasslands, reminded her friend.

They were in the drawing-room having just completed a tour of the house and the grounds.

'Do you know – I know it's a silly question but life is full of extraordinary coincidences – do you know Yuichi Matsumoto, Mr Bennet? He comes from Tokyo.'

'I'm afraid I don't, Mrs Lane.'

An idea suddenly came to Barbara. 'My aunt who lived in Hove died recently—'

'I'm sorry to hear that,' said Matthew, formally.

'She was as old as the hills. She died while posing for a portrait this Yuichi was painting of her. You may have noticed the picture when we were in the study.'

'Yes, I did,' replied Matthew. 'Rather striking, I thought.'

'It's the portrait of my aunt painted by Yuichi. Quite something, I'd say, and what a wonderful way to die! While you're being made immortal! She died of a heart attack, quite painlessly. Yuichi went on painting her for some time before he realised what had happened. Anyway, I didn't mean to talk about the dramatic death of my aunt, what I was going to say was that living in the same block of flats was the mother of a woman who teaches in Tokyo. Her name is Sylvia something—'

'Sylvia Field. I happen to know her well. She's a great friend,' said Matthew, who liked to be able to claim a female acquaintance when in normal society.

'There! Didn't I say that life was full of extraordinary coincidences. Cecily?'

Cecily had begun a conversation with Matthew's sister.

'What's that, dear?' asked Cecily.

'Nothing, just a coincidence.'

Cecily returned to her conversation.

'I know I shouldn't ask you this question, Mr Bennet, as it's none of my business, but are you retiring soon?'

'It's odd that you should ask me that, Mrs Lane. I was thinking of retiring, but I've changed my mind, at least I think I've changed my mind.' Matthew uttered a weak laugh.

'Because if you bought this place, you could hardly leave it empty. It would be taken over by squatters in no time, and it would be hard to get them out, wouldn't it Cecily?'

'Wouldn't what?' She again broke off her stream of talk; she seemed to be getting on well with Mary.

'I was telling Mr Bennet that if this house was left empty it would be invaded by the homeless.'

'Not if the gardener and his wife were here. They've kept the raiders at bay before when you've been away, and you have an alarm system.' Cecily resumed her confabulation.

'Oh, I forgot to tell you about the alarm system, Mr Bennet,' Barbara said. 'It's connected to the police station. Would you like to see how it works?'

'Well, I don't think that would serve any purpose at the moment. You see, I haven't quite made up my mind about the house. I thought I might have a sort of school for Japanese students who need to improve their English before going on to a university.' This idea had just occurred to Matthew.

'What a splendid scheme!' Barbara exclaimed. 'The house would certainly lend itself to such a project. Now, I think that the gardener and his wife would stay on. The cottage, it's a modern bungalow, really, as you may have noticed, has been their home for twenty years. Would you like to meet them?'

'I don't think that that would be necessary now, not yet

anyway. I shall have to think things over. There is the price—'

'Yes?' said Barbara, bristling, 'What about it?'

'I find it a bit high.' Matthew was beginning to wish that his sister had not dragged him into this house-viewing expedition. The idea, though, of having a school for Japanese students was starting to appeal to him. Jun could be the co-director. Mary seemed to have lost interest in the house now that she had seen it. She was absorbed in talking with Barbara's friend.

'I could make it less,' said Barbara, recklessly.

'Oh?'

'I could reduce the price by fifty thousand, perhaps.'

'That would make it four hundred and fifty thousand.'

'Which is nothing these days,' said Barbara, unconsciously imitating the way her son talked about money.

'To me it would be a great deal.'

'It's a very fine place. Unique. There are frequent trains to London and here you are really in the country. Shopping is easy if you have a car. There's a supermarket only three miles away.' She surprised herself by her own sales talk. 'Would you want any of the furniture? I must get rid of some of it. I'd rather like to feel that some of the old pieces would stay where they've been for years.'

'Um, I'm not sure. Well, Mrs Lane, thank you very much.' Matthew rose.

'Won't you have a drink?'

'Er, I'm not sure that we have time.' He glanced at his sister across the room locked in chatter – what could she be talking about? 'Mary,' he cried, and when she looked up he gave her a signal with his head that it was time to go. She took up her handbag and rose.

'I insist on your having a drink,' said Barbara. Cecily gave her a puzzled regard, raising one eyebrow and wrinkling her forehead.

'It's very kind of you.' Matthew and Mary sat down again.

'Gin and tonic? Campari soda? Sherry? White wine? What will it be?'

They all opted for gins and tonic.

While Barbara was out of the room fetching glasses, ice and lemon, Mary said to her brother, 'You seem to be getting on like a house on fire. Have you made an offer?'

'Not really.' Matthew wondered if his sister were serious or just keeping up the pretence.

When Barbara had poured out the drinks and handed them round, she raised her glass, 'Here's hoping you'll be happy here, Mr Bennet.'

Embarrassed, Matthew replied, 'Thank you. But it's a bit premature to say that, Mrs Lane.'

'I have a feeling that the place will soon be yours. I can hear eager Japanese students scampering about the house already. I might come down a little more.'

'Oh?'

'Another fifty thousand, perhaps?'

'That makes it very tempting.'

'I shall have to square it with the agent.'

They finished their drinks and Barbara saw Matthew and his sister into the little white car.

'I wish I had a car like that,' said Barbara to Matthew as he was adjusting his seat belt. Mary was at the wheel. 'So easy for parking.'

'Thank you again, Mrs Lane. Goodbye for now.'

'Goodbye. I'll speak to my agent and my solicitor on Monday.' Barbara waved until they had gone round the bend in the drive and were out of sight.

'I did my bit, didn't I Mary?'

'You went much farther than I expected you to. You really seem to have made her think you were serious about buying the place.'

Matthew giggled boyishly. 'She came down a hundred thousand. I told her the house would make a wonderful school for Japanese students and I thought of opening one. She believed me.'

'That's why she said she could already hear Japanese students scampering about the place. I wondered what she meant. She seemed a bit bonkers to me.'

'You got on very well with her friend. What on earth were you talking about, so intently.'

'She's a reader for a publisher and she reviews books. She's intelligent, very, and interested in history like me. We talked of Tuchman and Wedgwood, their books on the Middle Ages and the Thirty Years War.'

As soon as Barbara had regained the drawing-room, she let out a gale of laughter. 'He really thought I was serious,' she spluttered. 'I came down a hundred thousand and he thought I meant it.' She sat down and continued to laugh.

'It's not like you, Barbara, to tease a stranger.'

Between bursts of mirth, Barbara said, 'He talked about turning the house into a school for Japanese students . . . oh, it was so funny. I knew from the start he wasn't a serious purchaser; no one serious about buying a place would arrive in a car like that, so I egged him on. As if anyone would come down a hundred thousand! A silly man, and obviously a pansy; a poof, Neville would call him.'

'Are you going to make an offer then?' asked Mary of her brother as they were driving back to Chiddingfold.

'Of course not. I shall, though, mull over the idea of having a school for Japanese students when I retire. I know a Japanese who might help, and you, perhaps, could come in on it too.'

7

Trevor soon discovered that a hundred thousand pounds wasn't nearly enough to buy a flat, even a small one, in a central district. Having lived in luxury with Leonard in Rutland Gate he could not bear the thought of being out in the suburbs like his parents. He didn't fancy getting a mortgage. His father's advice never to borrow given when he was a child had stuck in his mind, so instead of raising a loan from a building society, he put £50,000 into one and the other half of the gift on deposit in his bank. He had talked to Wilson about his accommodation problem and had been advised to rent a place. He followed this advice by renting a furnished basement flat near Earls Court Station. Wilson was kind and was willing to lend a sympathetic ear when Trevor visited him in the shop during his lunch hour. The lonely young man asked Wilson if it would be a good idea to give up his job at the Oxford Street store and spend some of Leonard's money travelling; he wanted to go to Thailand, to Chiang Mai. Wilson, a cautious man, persuaded Trevor not to resign. He suggested that Trevor should ask his manager if he could take his annual holiday in December–January and go to Thailand then. Wilson was not mischievous; he did not mean to be instrumental in engineering an embarrassing confrontation between Leonard and Trevor; on the contrary, being romantic, he thought that a chance meeting in Chiang Mai might bring about a reconciliation. He felt sorry for Trevor.

8

'So you went to that sordid bar,' said Matthew to Jun disapprovingly, although in the past Matthew had patronised the place. 'Who's this Japanese you met?'

Jun told him about Yuichi, but not that he had spent the night in Leonard's flat; he only admitted to having lunched there on Sunday.

'A bisexual. I've never liked bisexuals, never trusted them. They're just out for sex, whichever kind comes their way, and they're out for whatever they can get out of it. They don't know what love is. The only person they ever love is themselves.'

It was noon on Monday. Matthew had just returned to Gordon Mansions and Jun had recounted his meeting with Yuichi and Leonard, omitting the details.

'And this Leonard, who's he?'

Jun told him what he knew about the rich bonviveur and his luxurious apartment. 'He wants to meet you,' said Jun.

'Why on earth should he?'

'I don't know. He just said he'd like to. "Please bring your friend next time," he said.'

'It sounds like one of those insincere invitations one gets from acquaintances who say, "You must come to dinner" and then they never fix a date, or ring up or anything.'

'I don't think he's like that,' said Jun.

In spite of Matthew's doubt, Leonard did telephone Jun and invite the couple to dinner on the following Saturday, the day before they were to fly back to Japan. Yuichi, to Barbara's dismay, had taken another weekend off from Grasslands and was present together with Wilson, at the party.

Barbara was sorely put out. She had sensed Yuichi's dislike of Cecily and had specifically asked her friend not to come down for the weekend. Yuichi was now attending an art school in London and commuting every day. He drove Barbara's Honda or her husband's Mercedes (he preferred to drive the latter) to Guildford and took the train from there, just as Henry had done. He would come back in the evening tired and not always in a pliable mood, which meant he did not visit her bedroom. She had been hoping that the Saturday and Sunday would turn out to be two days of bliss, but he had again gone off to spend the weekend with Leonard. She was jealous.

Matthew's reservations about Leonard evaporated when he met him. He was respectful (it was the respect of the bourgeois for the rich and the grand) and ingratiating towards his host, and was fascinated by Yuichi, who adopted the charming, alluring manner which had captivated Leonard, Jennifer, Barbara and Winifred. Jun seemed drawn to Wilson; they got on at once.

It being a Saturday, a servantless day, Leonard, with no apologies, served the meal in the kitchen, a room that contained paintings, porcelain and pottery ornaments that many a collector would be proud to display in the best room in the house. With envy Matthew noticed the Picasso prints and the paintings by John Minton and Keith Vaughan. On a shelf there was a Thai *bencharong* bowl similar to one Matthew gave pride of place to in his Tokyo apartment.

Leonard provided a chicken and rice dish and then, after cheese, crème caramel, and with it they drank Pouilly Fuissée. 'Not cooked by me,' Leonard informed his guests. 'My housekeeper made it and instructed me how to warm it up, and Yuichi did the rice in the rice cooker.'

The round kitchen table was spread with a batik cloth; the kitchen itself was impressively large. Yuichi, acting as if he were a member of the household, helped serve the food. Leonard talked of Chiang Mai and the house he had rented there. He also mentioned Jennifer and her Thai friend, not perhaps remembering that Yuichi had been Jennifer's lover and dismissed by her; the Japanese gave no sign of embarrassment.

'I shall go back in September or October,' said Leonard. 'Why don't you all come out for Christmas? Wilson is coming, aren't you, Wilson?'

'I didn't know I was.'

'Of course you are. Yuichi says he has to go back to Japan to see his parents but he could spend a few days in Chiang Mai on the way to Tokyo,' and turning to Matthew, he added, 'You and Jun could easily go over to Thailand from Tokyo.'

'I'm not so sure about that,' said Matthew, not one to agree on the spot to a suggestion that would involve the expenditure of a sizeable amount; the trip to London with Jun had cost a lot; he would need to recoup his finances before embarking on another one.

'I never been to Chiang Mai. I want to go there,' said Jun to Wilson. 'You will go?'

'Leonard seems to think so,' smiled Wilson.

Matthew frowned at his friend.

163

9

When the rains began in June the heat in Chiang Mai abated slightly. Jennifer, an energetic woman, was getting bored with her routine: shopping, swimming, lunching in the house, resting, tussling with a Thai textbook, and waiting for Somsak to turn up, which he didn't always do.

One morning in the Central supermarket, while searching for marmalade, she met an American woman who told her she ran a business that sold Thai antiques, modern furniture and lamps. She was about forty-five and was called Ann Sutton. Her partner was an Australian who had been her lover for a few years but had gone off to greener pastures. He appeared now and then to supervise the business at which he was brilliant and to pocket some of the profits and then disappeared again for months at a time. Ann was impressed by Jennifer's experience in antiques in the Oxford Street Store where Trevor worked, and persuaded Jennifer over a cup of coffee in a café in the same building as the supermarket to help out in the shop. Jennifer agreed to put in three days a week, which by the end of August had increased to four.

This occupation made all the difference to Jennifer's life in Chiang Mai. She had an interest, apart from Somsak and trying to learn Thai. She enjoyed the days when she had to go to the shop, which was on the left bank of the River Ping and on the other side of the city from the Golden Plaza. On her working days a *tuk-tuk* would arrive outside her house at half-past eight. Kom, the driver, a grizzled old man, was usually on time, but on some mornings he didn't turn up and Jennifer had to take one of the other motor-bicycle taxis which could be found waiting on the other side of the road. These drivers were more familiar than old Kom, who had told her he was sixty-three; they would whirl her down Huey Kaew Road weaving in and out of the traffic. They disregarded her cry of '*Cha-cha*' – slow. Kom obeyed the command and kept to a dignified pace; he would say 'sorry' when they went over a bump. Jennifer never tired of the part of the road which ran along the moat of the north side of the old city, in which at intervals fountains played and boys fished or swam. At the end there were the remains of the fortification of the ancient wall. Then Jennifer's journey became less interesting. They passed an ugly block, a hotel that catered for low-price package tours, a petrol station, and several business premises, then the forbidding wall of the American Consulate and finally at the top of the road by the River Ping was a holy *chedi*, round which the *tuk-tuk* had to drive before proceeding to Nawarat Bridge; on the right was an open market made colourful by the melons, the papaya, tomatoes, bananas and flowers. There was a clutter of jostling vehicles: trucks unloading produce from the fertile plain around Chiang Mai, red pick-ups that served as taxis dropping or taking on board passengers, cars, pedicabs and *tuk-tuks*. Jennifer was relieved when Kom had negotiated his way through this wheeled muddle and they had turned on to Nawarat Bridge over the sluggish, brown river on which clumps of water-hyacinth drifted almost imperceptibly down stream.

    Kom would return to fetch Jennifer from the shop at six o'clock and she would pay him three hundred *baht*, which Ann said was far too much. When Ann had warned Jennifer that she couldn't afford to pay her much, Jennifer replied that she would accept whatever she was able to pay her as the job was more important to her than the money; she needed something to do.

    On the days when Kom failed to call at her house in the morning he would usually arrive at the shop in the evening, his bloodshot eyes and tired, lined face betrayed the previous night's indulgence.

    Jennifer was happy.

10

Assembled for one of Neville's and Veronica's dinner parties were Barbara, Cecily, Wilson and Yuichi, who since Leonard's departure for Chiang Mai now spent every night of the week at Grasslands to Barbara's satisfaction. 'I must bring him,' Barbara had told Veronica on the phone. 'I hate driving at night and he drives so well, and when it's an evening engagement I prefer to come up by car.' Reluctantly, Veronica, who disliked the Japanese, thinking him venal, had agreed.

Robert, the baby, now eighteen months old, had been displayed and admired in the appropriate manner. Yuichi showed the Japanese liking for small children by fawning over the baby more than any of the others, including the grandmother. To Veronica's distaste her little son seemed to be attracted to Yuichi and beamed at him. When Barbara picked up the toddling infant, he had yelled and stretched out his chubby arms towards Yuichi, and when she had passed the baby to the Japanese his crying stopped.

'The charm works even with tots,' Wilson whispered to Cecily.

The baby was now back in his cot. Over the pork casserole Barbara recounted, not for the first time, the visit to Grasslands by Matthew and his sister, Mary. 'He really thought I was serious when I came down a hundred thousand. It was a scream. I can now tell whether a prospective buyer is genuine. Often people come to view the house merely to satisfy their curiosity. I guessed at once that Mr Bennet and his sister fell into that category. People see the ad in *Country Life* or outside the agent's office and arrange to visit the place.'

'Mother,' said Neville,' you really ought to complain to the agent and tell him to vet viewers properly.'

'Actually, I rather enjoy the visits,' Barbara admitted. 'They break the monotony. Leonard Crampstead came, but really to see Yuichi, not me or the house, although I had met him before in Chiang Mai.'

They all regarded the Japanese, who took up his glass of red wine.

'Talking of Chiang Mai,' Barbara continued, 'I hear,' she looked at Yuichi, who was sitting opposite her, 'that Leonard is already there in his rented house, which is next to Jennifer's. And, did I tell you, Jennifer's got a job in a shop selling antiques, just up her street.'

'I fear for my sister,' said Neville. 'No good will come of this protracted stay in Thailand.'

'She might,' put in Cecily, 'become knowledgeable about Thai antiques and that could perhaps be useful in the future.'

No one contributed towards this suggestion. Veronica rose to collect the plates. Yuichi started to get up to help her, but she declined his offer and he sat down again.

'You are coming with me to Chiang Mai for Christmas, aren't you, Neville?'

'I don't think so, Mother.'

'Oh, but you must. Christmas Day will be the first anniversary of your father's death. We must be there to put flowers on his grave and say a prayer. I've written to Arthit and asked him to come up to Chiang Mai, and Jennifer will be there, of course. Arthit has left the firm and he and his wife with the help of Henry's legacy, I presume, have started a restaurant. The wife is Chinese, you know, and they are good at restaurants. Peter Cochrane will be away. He told me in a letter that he was going to Australia. We don't need him, and we don't need that funny little priest either. Veronica could come with us.'

Veronica returned from the kitchen with plates and a large glass bowl. 'What could Veronica do?' she asked.

'Go to Chiang Mai with us,' replied Barbara.

'And what about Robert?'

'Couldn't your parents look after him?'

'It'd be too much for them.'

'We wouldn't be away for long. We could stay with Jennifer. She says she has only basic comforts but the house has three bedrooms and two bathrooms.' Without waiting for her daughter-in-law to answer she turned and spoke to Wilson, who was next to her. 'And are you going to Chiang Mai?'

'I said I'd join Leonard and he's offered to put me up in his house.'

'So we'll all be there. It'll be fun,' exclaimed Barbara. 'What about you Cecily?'

'No, definitely not, count me out. Wild horses couldn't drag me there.'

'And Yuichi? You said something about going with us to Thailand on your way to Tokyo.'

'Yes. I go to Japan to see my father and my mother and maybe I stop in Chiang Mai on the way to Tokyo.'

Barbara stretched out a leg and rubbed Yuichi's calf with the toe of her shoe.

Veronica, having passed round the pudding-plates, gave the bowl of wine cream to Cecily, who helped herself and handed it across the table to Wilson.

'What's this?' asked Barbara as Wilson was holding the bowl out to her.

'Wine cream,' said Veronica.

Barbara took two large spoonfuls of the pudding and passed it to Yuichi after Wilson had taken a modest helping.

'It's really good, Veronica,' she said. 'You must give me the recipe.' The Japanese refused the cream and handed the bowl to Neville. 'Aren't you having any, Yuichi,' asked Barbara.

'I do not much like sweet thing,' stated Yuichi, apologetically.

'I thought you did,' said Barbara, trying to rub his leg again.

'What are you doing, Mother?' asked Neville. 'That's my leg.'

'Oh!'

11

'I can't possibly let you take your holiday over the Christmas and New Year period,' said Mr Cutler, manager of the Display Department of the Oxford Street store to Trevor. 'It's the busiest time of the year. You know that.'

'The windows are all finished,' said Trevor.

'They're done for Christmas, but not for the New Year and the Sales.'

'Then I'll resign,' said Trevor petulantly, thinking of the large sum in his bank.

'Don't be an idiot, Trevor. You'd find it hard to get another job.'

'I won't need one.'

'What d'you mean? Have you come into money or something?'

'Yes, I 'ave,' said Trevor defiantly.

Disconcerted by Trevor's smug expression, the manager, not an unkind man, said, 'Now look, you know we need every hand we've got at this time of the year but—'

'I've made up my mind. Sorry. I won't be comin' in tomorrow.'

'Look, I'll tell you what I'll do. I'll fix it so that you can take your holiday in February after the Sales are over.'

'Won't do, I'm afraid. Sorry. It's now or never.'

Mr Cutler began to get annoyed by Trevor's truculence. 'You'll miss your bonus if you walk out now,' he warned.

'I don't care. I won't need it.' Trevor, a weak man trying to be strong, rashly went farther than he intended; after all, Leonard would still be in Chiang Mai in February.

'I hope the fortune you've apparently inherited,' said Mr Cutler, middle aged and burdened with a feckless wife and three small daughters, 'is at least in six figures. These days, what appears to be a lot often isn't all that much, you know.'

'It is in six figures as a matter of fact.' Trevor didn't divulge that it only just reached that mark.

'Well, Trevor, it's your life. You must do as you like with it. I think, though, that you're acting very unwisely.'

'That's up to me isn't it?'

'Yes, it's up to you.' Cutler was too mild a man to maintain an angry stance, but solemnly said, 'You're letting us down, you know, and I don't like that.'

'That's too bad.' Trevor stalked out of the manager's inner office, gathered up his things and went out into freezing Oxford Street, saying goodbye to a few astonished colleagues on the way.

He broke his journey home by calling in at a travel agent and booked a flight to Chiang Mai via Bangkok and a room in the Golden Plaza. The return date was left open. Why shouldn't he spend the winter in the sun like Leonard? He could afford to now.

12

At one p.m. two days before Christmas Day, Leonard and Jennifer were waiting at Chiang Mai airport for the plane from Bangkok, which was to bring Barbara, Neville, Wilson and Yuichi. Jennifer had not set eyes on Yuichi since she had made her midnight flit from Grasslands on the previous Christmas Eve, having seen him and Trevor rolling about on the floor. She had heard from Leonard, not from her mother, that Yuichi had been staying at Grasslands, and she presumed that he and Barbara had done some bedding down together. She didn't care now that she had Somsak, who, unlike Yuichi, was, at heart, a simple, guileless soul. Jennifer had decided to act towards her young, lustful ex-lover, as if she had never met him; she would be correctly polite.

The plane also had Trevor as a passenger, but so far he had not been noticed by the others. The plane was full and while Trevor was in Economy Class, the Lane contingent and Wilson were travelling in Royal Orchid Executive Class.

Although after their fight they had made up their quarrel, which Trevor had begun by calling Yuichi 'a fucking Jap', Trevor was a bit nervous of Yuichi.

'Will they have done their Immigration and Customs checks in Bangkok or will they have to do it here?' Leonard asked Jennifer.

'I've no idea.'

'Because if they've done their checks in Bangkok, they'll come through this, the Domestic, exit, but if they haven't they'll come through the exit at the other end, right over there.' Leonard pointed down the vast airport hall.

'You go to that end,' said Jennifer, 'and I'll wait here. If they come out at that end, bring them over here.'

Leonard agreed and set off towards the far end of the hall.

The plane's arrival was shown on the television screens, but neither Leonard at his end nor Jennifer at hers could see the passengers walking from the plane to the Arrival Hall or waiting round the luggage carousel for their bags. At last, at Jennifer's end, Barbara, Yuichi, Wilson and Neville appeared, Yuichi and Neville pushing trolleys.

Two hundred yards away at Leonard's end out of the curtained glass door came Trevor.

'Good Lord,' exclaimed Leonard, 'you!'

'Yes, it's me, Leonard. Come to see what goes on in Chiang Mai.'

'Where are you staying?'

'At a hotel called the Golden Plaza. Do you know it?' Trevor had been told of the hotel by Wilson.

'Yes of course I know it. I'm staying there myself, or at least in one of the houses belonging to it. You'll find the hotel bus outside. I'm waiting for some friends.' Leonard waved towards the exit.

'See you.' Trevor wheeled his trolley away.

Leonard waited at the International Exit, but none of the others emerged. He peeped through the curtained door and saw there were no other passengers left at the Immigration check point, and the moving luggage band was still. He returned to the Domestic section, where he found Jennifer chatting merrily to her mother and brother, while Wilson and Yuichi stood aside, not wishing to intrude upon the family reunion. After welcoming the new arrivals, Leonard said, 'We'd better take two taxis. Jennifer, you and your family can go together, and I'll take Wilson and Yuichi.'

It had been arranged for Wilson and Yuichi to stay with Leonard, and Barbara and her son with Jennifer. Barbara would have liked Yuichi to be in the same house as herself, but in view of Jennifer's previous relations with the young Japanese and her own recent intimacy with him – it was better that he wasn't; nevertheless she was envious of Leonard's having him under his roof. She wished that Yuichi hadn't come to Chiang Mai. His presence was disturbing.

Yuichi took the seat by the driver, while Leonard and Wilson sat in the back of the taxi.

'Trevor's here,' said Leonard to Wilson.

'No! Is he really?'

'I was expecting you, Barbara and the others to appear and who should do so but Trevor. I nearly fell over.'

'Did he speak to you?'

'Yes. He said in that mock deferential manner, which he used to put on sometimes and which I found intensely irritating, that he'd come to see what goes on in Chiang Mai. I don't know what he meant exactly; a *double entendre* I suppose, meaning also what I was up to. And he's staying at the Golden Plaza, if you please. He's digging into that money I gave him, no doubt.'

'You'll have to see him.' Wilson smiled.

'I shall be coldly polite.'

13

The phone rang in Sylvia's Tokyo flat. She knew it was Toshi. They usually spoke to each other around seven on alternate days. When Toshi was in Tokyo they had spoken almost every day before he had gone to live with her, but now he was in Saga they had reduced their calls to three times a week. It was Christmas Eve and Toshi had rung to give her his greetings.

'Thanks. Sweet of you to call, darling,' said Sylvia. 'Now, about Chiang Mai, I've made all the arrangements. We'll fly there on the twenty-eighth with Matthew and Jun. We won't stop in Bangkok. We'll just change planes there and fly on up to—'

'I am very sorry, Siru-san, I cannot go with you.'

'Cannot go? But I've made all the bookings – at least Matthew has. We don't need visas for a short stay.'

'I cannot leave my office till thirty December and I mus' be back here at the bank on six January.'

'Oh darling, that's impossible. What can I do? What about your ticket?'

'Cancel.'

No amount of pleading could alter Toshi's decision and on the 28th December Sylvia, Matthew and Jun flew to Chiang Mai. 'What am I to do without Toshi?' Sylvia asked Matthew. 'We'd been planning this trip for weeks. When I saw him in Osaka last month, he was excited about going to Thailand, where he's never been.'

'Perhaps Chiang Mai will produce some sort of consolation,' said Matthew.

'What do you mean by that?' Sylvia snapped.

'Oh, nothing.'

14

'So you knew he was coming,' said Leonard.

He and Wilson were sitting under an umbrella by the

Golden Plaza pool; both of them were in swimming trunks, over which their stomachs bulged.

'Yes, more or less.'

'Why didn't you warn me?'

'I forgot. I've been so busy.'

'Very sly of you, Wilson.'

'Here he is now.'

'Oh God!'

Trevor arrived at the pool wearing a shirt with the buttons undone and brief bathing slips. He saw Leonard and Wilson at once, but did not go over to them; he took off his shirt and lay on a sun-bed.

'What shall I do?'

'Say hello, sweetly, and ask him to your party.'

'Don't want to.'

'Do you good to do something you don't want to do for a change.'

'Don't be bitchy, dear.'

Trevor dived into the water and started to swim lengths. He swam well.

'Can't talk to him while he's half submerged.'

'He'll surface soon.'

Trevor climbed out of the pool near where Leonard and Wilson were sitting. He went up to the two old men and greeted them politely, and, it seemed, without embarrassment. Wilson was impressed by the young man's apparent self-control. Leonard was flustered.

'How are you enjoying Chiang Mai?' asked Leonard.

'Not much. It's a dump.'

'I'm sorry you think that. If I had known you were coming, Trevor, I'd have offered you a bed. But my house is full now. Sorry about that. I'm giving a small party on the thirty-first, evening, around eight. Please come to it, if you're still here.'

'Thanks. I shall be. I'm going on a trip to another town called Chiang something to see a river, but only for two days.'

'You mean Chiang Rai and the Mekong. Are you going there alone?'

'No, with two old English queens I met in the bar.'

'Oh?'

'See you.' Trevor slipped back to his sun-bed and lay on his stomach.

'Would you really have put Trevor up if you'd known he was coming here?' asked Wilson.

'No. But there was no harm in my saying so when it wasn't feasible. The offer, I thought, showed I had no hard feelings.'

'What an old devil you are, Leonard.'

'Aren't I? I wonder who the two old queens are?'

'You're not jealous, are you?'

'Course not. It probably isn't true, anyway.'

15

On the morning of December the 29th the sexagenarian couple were again sitting by the pool, again in swimming shorts, again talking about Trevor. Wilson was trying to persuade Leonard to see the young man. Barbara, Neville, Jennifer, Matthew, Jun and Sylvia appeared on the scene, all dressed for a swim. Leonard and Wilson hailed them loudly. Barbara had met Matthew in the lobby and at the same time was introduced to Sylvia and Jun. The trio from Tokyo had arrived in the evening of the previous day. Sylvia remembered that she had met Barbara's aunt in Hove and expressed her sorrow when she was told she had died.

At the pool, they joined Leonard and Wilson. The waiters with the fine calves were pleased to move tables, umbrellas and chairs for the new guests, who looked as if they would give good orders and tips.

Barbara found herself sitting next to Sylvia. She told her about her husband's death a year ago and that the main purpose of her present visit was to put flowers on Henry's grave. 'We did it on Christmas Day, the day he was killed last year. His friend, his devoted Thai friend, came up from Bangkok for the ceremony. It wasn't a ceremony really, just the placing of flowers and then two minutes of silence.'

'It's a sad visit for you then,' remarked Sylvia.

'Yes, in that respect. But I like it here. My daughter – she's over there talking to Leonard Crampstead – lives here. She has a job in a furniture shop. I wish she'd come home and live in England. She has a Thai boyfriend, a teacher of art.' Barbara looked over at Leonard. 'What have you done with Yuichi?'

'He's gone into town for shopping. You know how they love shopping.'

After the party had swum – Sylvia, Jun and Neville seriously, the others chatting as they floundered about – they returned to the shade of the umbrellas.

'So have you decided about the house, Mr Bennet?' Barbara teased. 'The agent told me he hadn't heard from you.'

'I've given it deep thought,' replied Matthew. 'I really liked the place very much. I think, though, with much regret I must say no. I may stay in Japan for a while longer.'

'I'm sorry to hear that. I was almost sure you were a serious purchaser.'

'What are we going to do about lunch?' asked Matthew, hoping that the mention of food would divert Barbara away from any more references to Grasslands.

'Let's have it here,' suggested Sylvia. 'I saw the menu at the bar. It looks tempting.'

16

Leonard, taking Wilson's advice, contacted Trevor in the hotel and invited him round to his house on the morning of the thirty-first of December, when Wilson and Yuichi had gone to the mountain temple of Doi Suthep, a 'must' according to the guidebook. His recent life among the rich and the blasé had not damped Yuichi's Japanese enthusiasm for sightseeing.

Trevor arrived, dressed in a black T-shirt embossed with the head of Elvis Presley in gold, slacks, and flip-flops.

Leonard said, 'Good God! Where on earth did you get that shirt?'

'Night Market.'

'Whatever persuaded you to buy it?'

'Don't you like it?'

'Of course I don't.'

'I thought you would. Your style.'

Leonard, determined not to be provoked by Trevor's offensive manner, said courteously, 'What may I offer you to drink?'

'It's a bit early for a drink, isn't it? It's only ten.'

'Coffee, then, orange juice?'

'No, thanks.'

At first they exchanged banalities about Chiang Mai, the trip to Chiang Rai and the Mekong River, the Golden Plaza and Leonard's rented house, about which Trevor said, 'Bit of a come-down after Rutland Gate, isn't it?'

'The climate makes up for the inconvenience,' replied Leonard tartly.

The tartness raised Trevor's hackles. 'I 'ear you 'ave a Thai lover.'

'Wilson told you, I suppose.' Leonard knew perfectly well that the dropping of the aitches was done on purpose to annoy him, but he kept his temper; he didn't want to quarrel; the idea of the meeting was to try and have a sort of reconciliation with the young man.

'Right,' said Trevor, and then, looking down and obviously making an effort, he continued, 'I suppose I must thank you for that money you gave me. I thought I'd give it back at first, but I've decided to keep it. I've resigned from the store. Decided to live it up a bit.'

'Very foolish of you. My idea was for you to buy a flat with the money, not to squander it on extravagant trips. You can give it back, if you like. I won't feel snubbed should you do so.'

'I've rented a flat and put half the money into a Building Society, and the rest is in my bank. Flats cost so much; those in upmarket districts, that is.'

Leonard didn't say that an 'upmarket' district hadn't been in his mind when he made the gift. He said firmly, 'I can't afford to give you any more. I had to make sacrifices to provide you with that sum.'

Trevor, who knew this wasn't the exact truth, mumbled, 'Good of you. Did you invite me round to tell me that?'

'I wanted to talk to you, Trevor.'

'What about?'

'I want us to remain friends. I would like to see you now and then.'

'That's good of you.' There was sarcasm in Trevor's tone.

'Don't be bitter. You ran out on me.'

'You gave me cause.'

'Don't let's go into all that. It's past.' Looking at Trevor, pink from the sun, nose peeling, red, hairy forearms, Leonard wondered how he had ever had an affair with him; compared with Amnuay, he was now quite unalluring; the attraction which he had once had had evaporated; love had not turned to hatred but to indifference. 'Please remember that if you need advice, you can call on me. I'm sorry you've given up your job. A pity. But that's your business.' Leonard rose; he was embarrassed. Trevor jumped to his feet. 'Well?' said Leonard dismissively.

'OK,' returned Trevor.

'You will come to my party tonight, won't you? Just to show there is no ill feeling.'

'I don't know about there being no ill feeling, but I'll come to your party 'cause I said I would. Can I go out the back way? It's a shorter way back to the hotel, I guess.'

'You're right. It is.' Leonard went ahead across the room and opened the backdoor. 'Mind that gutter; it's easy to trip into it, if you're not careful.'

'Thanks.' Trevor left.

Leonard sighed. 'Have I been a swine?' he asked himself aloud. 'I did give him a hundred thousand pounds. What an idiot to give up his job! It's my fault, I suppose. Money spoils people, even the best.'

17

'Will your friend – what's his name?'

'Somsak,' Jennifer reminded her mother irritably.

'Will Somsak be coming to Leonard's New Year's Eve party tonight?'

'No. he would hate it. He's shy.'

'It's silly to be shy. Shy people miss so much. Jennifer, are you really going to stay on in Chiang Mai?'

'Yes. I like it here. I have a job now and I feel that Somsak needs me. I want to help him.'

'How?'

'With his painting.'

'That's the second painter you've got mixed up with.'

'He's different; truer; simpler; he doesn't sleep around, I'm sure.'

'Are you going to marry him?'

'No, I don't think so. He doesn't want to get married.'

'Well, that's something.' Barbara paused and then said, 'Jennifer, I shall go to Bangkok tomorrow, or the next day.'

'Oh, Mummy, why?'

'I want to see Arthit. He rushed off back to Bangkok after the little remembrance ceremony at Henry's grave. I hardly had a word with him.'

'Why should you want to see him?'

'I want to find out what your father saw in him. I want to know what he has and I obviously haven't.'

'What he has, Mummy darling, is a prick. Daddy was gay. You know that.'

'I want to be better acquainted with the man Henry cared for. I want to understand Henry's infatuation.'

'Mummy, you're crazy.'

'Maybe. But I shall go to Bangkok tomorrow or the next day.' Barbara didn't add that she had thought much about her husband's Thai lover and felt that she would be nearer to Henry, whom she had truly loved and whom she loved more now he was dead than when he was alive, if she could go to bed with Arthit. Yuichi had just been a temporary pastime, an aberration. She knew he never really cared for her. He had obliged because of her kindness to him, a way of paying for his accommodation at Grasslands; and he had slaked his lust when there was no one else around. The last time he had slept with her the fire had gone out of his lovemaking; she had felt it was a duty performance. Now in Chiang Mai were Leonard and her daughter. Although Jennifer had lost interest in Yuichi, Leonard probably hadn't. Barbara did not want to appear in competition with the satyric, egocentric millionaire. Yuichi might try to play her off against him; she certainly didn't want that.

18

'Is Mr Banana coming to the party tonight?' asked Wilson. It was five o'clock and they were having tea, which Wilson had made, on the verandah of Leonard's house.

'Oh, don't call him Mr Banana. It's so patronising, making him out to be a sort of joke.'

'You used to.'

'Only at the beginning. I call him by his name which is Amnuay. He came to see me this afternoon while you were resting and Yuichi went to the pool when you got back from Doi Suthep. Did you walk up all those steps?'

'No. We took the funicular up and walked down.'

'The funicular sometimes breaks down, you know.'

'It worked all right this morning. It was too misty to have a good view of Chiang Mai.'

'That's usual at this time of the year. To answer your question: no, Amnuay is not coming to the party.'

'Why not? Did you put him off because of Yuichi?'

'No. Yuichi wouldn't have minded. He's got his eye on that woman who came from Japan. I think he went to the pool to meet her.' Leonard sipped his tea, and putting down his cup resumed, 'Amnuay isn't coming to the party because he doesn't drink and I know he would not enjoy a crowd of foreigners.'

'Did you see Trevor?'

'Yes. He came round this morning.'

'How did you get on with him?'

'Not well. It was a meeting wrought with disharmony. I tried my best to be conciliatory—'

'Ha!' said Wilson.

Leonard frowned and went on, 'He remained resentful in spite of the hundred thousand pounds. He did have the courtesy to thank me for it, albeit in a decidedly off hand manner. I was shocked to hear he's given up his job.'

'Oh dear, has he really? I didn't know.'

'Why on earth did you suggest to him that he came here?' Leonard asked with displeasure in his voice.

'I had an idea, and I've had it all along, ever since your break-up with him, that there might be a reconciliation, that you'd have him back.'

'Do-gooders get things wrong. I have no intention of having him back. You persuaded me to give him that money, which was far too big a sum for me to part with and for him to handle, by playing on my guilty feelings and my good nature, and that is that. I did tell him I'd help him, with advice, should he need it in future. The affair is over and it's none of your business to try to revive it. I offered him friendship and he more or less scorned my offer.' Leonard again sipped his tea. 'It's gone cold,' he said, 'And another thing, Wilson, why did you tell him I had a Thai lover?'

'Did I? I'd forgotten I had. It must have slipped out during one of his lunch-hour visits to my shop. I'm sorry Leonard. I was only doing what I thought was best.'

'Good intentions, Wilson, good intentions, so often misconceived.'

'Is he coming to your party?'

'He said he would with what one might call insolent reluctance. And he was wearing the most frightful T-shirt, black and emblazoned in gold with the head of Elvis Presley. Put on, no doubt, expressly to annoy me.'

'Oh dear!'

'Yes, oh dear Wilson. Your fatuous attempt at do-goodery has caused nothing but embarrassment and probably wrecked Trevor's life. He'll never get as good a job.'

'Oh dear, I'm sorry.'

'Yes, Wilson, oh dear! And again oh dear!'

19

'Neville, you must go to Leonard's party,' said Barbara to her son. 'He's gone to such trouble, Jennifer says.'

'I'll look in for a bit. What sort of party is it going to be with three women and seven men?' They were downstairs in Jennifer's sitting-room.

'It'll be fun. Leonard's hired a band.'

'I believe that that appalling ex-boyfriend of Leonard's will be there – Trevor something.'

'I don't know him.'

'He works in the store Jennifer used to work in. She made me drive him down to Grasslands for the Christmas party last year, that terrible day when in the middle of lunch we had a call from Bangkok to say that Father had been killed. He's a wretched little whining poof. I shall stay for a short time.'

Neville did not add that he was going to go off and find a Thai girl. One of the porters in the lobby had arranged for a *tuk-tuk* driver to take him somewhere around eight-thirty. 'This is the most uncomfortable sofa I've ever sat on,' Neville complained. 'It's like sitting on a sack of bones.'

'Why not sit in one of the chairs? They're slightly better.'

Neville moved to a chair. 'As you say, Mother, *slightly* better. Jennifer must be mad to stay in this awful place.'

'Shush,' said Barbara, putting a finger to her lips. 'She's just had a bath. She'll be down in a minute.'

'What should I wear for this wretched do of Crampstead's? A flamboyant old queen if ever there was one. I don't know why you get mixed up with all these dreadful people. Most of one's countrymen one meets abroad are the dregs. Should I wear a tie?'

'No, you'll do as you are. He said dress casually,' replied Barbara, 'which means, I suppose, just a shirt and slacks. That's what everyone wears here, except the manager who sweats about in a tie.'

'Talking of Thais – ha ha – there'll be none at the party as far as I can gather. Jennifer's boyfriend sensibly won't come, or she thinks he won't. Apparently the Thais have a way of saying "Yes" when they mean "No". It's hard for us poor Westerners to decipher their intentions.' To himself Neville wondered if the porter had really told the *tuk-tuk* driver what he wanted and if the driver would turn up.

'I wish Veronica were here,' said Barbara.

'So do I,' echoed her son, thinking about his rendezvous with the *tuk-tuk* driver. 'It's damnable that her parents wouldn't look after the brat. Veronica did spend Christmas with them. She told me on the phone just now.'

'I thought I heard you on the phone when I was upstairs dressing and I wondered. Why didn't you tell me, Neville? I would have liked to speak to her.'

'Why? You never cared for her.'

'Don't let's go into that now, for God's sake.' Barbara bridled. 'It's not true anyway.'

'Oh Mother!'

Jennifer descended the stairs. She was wearing a cornflower-blue dress with short sleeves, and a string of pearls. The blue showed off to advantage her unfashionably tidy head of blonde hair, cut in page-boy style, and matched her eyes; her figure was almost as slim as a Thai's.

'Where did you get that dress, Jennifer?' asked her mother.

'Here. A Chinese dressmaker.'

Barbara rose and examined the dress. 'Quite well made, not badly cut. How much?'

'About a hundred and fifty pounds.'

'Good heavens! So cheap? I must have one made at once.' Barbara looked again at her daughter's dress. 'Yes, dear, it's fine.' She touched the hem of the garment. 'A bit skimpy, perhaps.'

'I don't think so,' protested Jennifer.

'Possibly, it's rather long.'

'It's the length I wanted. I like your get-up, Mummy.'

'"Get-up" you call it? It cost the earth.' Barbara was wearing a fawn slim trouser suit whose collarless jacket hung loosely round her full figure; she had tied a yellow silk scarf round her neck to hide its stringiness.

'It's a bit pyjamaish,' said her daughter.

'Trouser suits aren't made to fit like gloves, darling. I asked for it to be an easy fit.'

'I wish you two,' said Neville, thinking of his rendezvous, 'would stop talking about clothes. We should go next door.'

'Next door?' said Barbara, surprised. 'Not to the hotel?'

'The party, Crampstead's party, is taking place in his quarters. They hardly deserve the name of house.'

20

Leonard had hired a little band, a trio of male students whom he had heard play at a restaurant not far from the Golden Plaza. The band consisted to two guitars and a clarinet. The clarinettist was also the vocalist. What attracted Leonard about the musicians were their looks and their repertoire, which, surprisingly, included numbers from the thirties, forties and fifties. It transpired that the three happened to like dated dance tunes from that period and went to some trouble to get hold of the music.

Barbara, Jennifer and Neville arrived just as the orchestra was preparing to begin their programme.

Leonard, in a jazzy batik shirt which hung outside his trousers, held a cigar in his left hand, a glass in his right; he came forward to greet them. 'How good of you to come,' he said fatuously. 'I think you know everyone here. The waiters will serve you.'

The others – Trevor, who had changed his black T-shirt for a white one which was printed with the words 'Something Special' in red letters, Matthew, Sylvia, Wilson, Yuichi and Jun – were standing about with glasses in their hands. The two waiters from the hotel passed round canapés and drinks: white wine, Campari or whisky and soda.

The band struck up 'You're the Cream in my Coffee.'

Barbara said to Leonard, 'How extraordinary to hear that tune.'

'I chose these boys because they know and they like old-fashioned numbers. I much prefer them.'

'So do I, so do I! But where did you find them?'

'They're from Chiang Mai University and they make a little money by playing at a restaurant up the road. I've engaged them for the evening. The restaurant will have to put up with canned music tonight. I'm giving them more than they usually get paid.'

The vocalist said, 'You the *cleam* in my coffee, you the milk in my tea.'

Leonard put his cigar in an ashtray, went to the centre of the room and clapped imperiously. 'Now everyone must dance, please.' He signalled to the waiters to gather the glasses. 'Choose your partners.' Leonard opened the ball with Barbara. The others hesitated. 'Now, come on please; never mind who you dance with.'

Yuichi chose Sylvia as his partner and she seemed pleased; Jennifer danced with Jun; Trevor stumbled about with Wilson, neither of them enjoying themselves; Neville slipped away; Matthew sat in a chair watching Jun, who was trying to jog with Jennifer.

While the trio was playing 'I Get a Kick out of You', Leonard, relinquishing Barbara, clapped his hands again. 'Everyone change partners, please.' Yuichi would not let Sylvia go and she stayed with him. Barbara went over to Matthew and pulled him to his feet; Jennifer approached Trevor, 'Come dance with me, Something Special.' 'I can't dance.' 'I'll show you.' Jun danced with Wilson.

'I get no keeck from cocaine,' sang the vocalist, perhaps untruthfully.

Leonard went into the kitchen to talk to the waiters.

Suddenly, the lights went out.

'Candles,' ordered Leonard. 'There are some, but where are they? There's one in my bedroom upstairs.'

'I get,' said a waiter.

'No, you don't know where.' Leonard flicked on his lighter and slowly mounted the steep stairs. Five dark minutes passed while he was fumbling round his dressing-table and before he had found the candle the lights came on again. He descended to the living-room. The band struck up with 'Smoke gets in Your Eyes'. All the guests except Matthew and Trevor had disappeared.

'Where has everyone gone?'

Gleefully, Trevor gabbled out, 'Wilson said something about taking Jun to a gay bar called "My Cup"; Yuichi and Sylvia went out the back way, to the hotel, I imagine.'

'And Barbara and Jennifer?'

'They've gone to Jennifer's house. I heard her say, "Come on, Mummy, let's go and have a talk."'

'How rude of them!'

'When laughing flends delide,' sang the vocalist, 'tears I cannot hide . . .'

'I've arranged for dinner,' moaned Leonard. 'It's all ready.'

'Let's have it,' said Trevor. 'I'm hungry.'

'I ordered dinner for ten. There are only three of us.'

'The waiters and the boys in the band could join us, couldn't they?' suggested Matthew.

'Excellent idea.' Leonard clapped his hands. 'Stop playing! Stop cooking! Stop waiting! Come and eat with us, all of you.' The trio and the waiters, after they had carried a number of Thai dishes from the kitchen to the dining-table, sat down and they all began to guzzle the food and quaff the wine or the whisky.

Matthew, sitting between the two waiters, was perfectly content, and so was Leonard with a member of the band on either side of him. Trevor acted stand-offishly, not fitting in with the company. The Thais were natural and uninhibited, eating and drinking voraciously.

'I'm delighted,' said Leonard, 'the others stole away. Our new companions are more congenial, more fun.' He eyed the waiter sitting opposite him across the table. 'Let's have a tune! Play orchestra, play!' Cheeks puce, eyes glinting, forehead beaded with perspiration, bald pate glowing, Leonard was well away in his cups.

The guitarists started to strum uncertainly; then the clarinettist struck up with 'I'm on a See-saw'. Leonard bawled, 'I adore this song. It comes from a musical comedy called . . . now what was it called? It was by Vivian Ellis, if I'm not mistaken.'

Out of tune Leonard croaked a couplet from the thirties' song: 'You throw me up and you throw me down, I don't know whether I'm here or there . . .' He roared with laughter. The waiters clapped. He reminded Matthew of an intoxicated Japanese businessman in a karaoke bar.

'It's New Year's Eve,' said Matthew in a bored voice. 'What shall we do at midnight? Dance again?'

'No, kiss,' hissed Leonard fiercely.

Trevor rose. 'I'm not going to fuckin' kiss anyone. I'm off,' he whined, adopting his south London accent to irritate Leonard, who leered at him fuzzily as he crossed the room to the front door. On the threshold Trevor turned, called out sarcastically, 'A 'appy New Year, then,' and disappeared into the dark lane.

'Well now,' said Leonard, 'perhaps it's time for bed.'

The waiters began to clear the table and the musicians to pack up their instruments. Leonard tottered to the head of the stairs and slowly began to ascend. Half way up, he looked over the banister and said to Matthew, who had moved to an armchair. 'Sorry to leave you all alone. I simply must go to bed. Please stay on as long as you wish. Get one of the waiters to give you a whisky.'

'Thanks.' Matthew sighed.

He soon fell asleep. At midnight he was awakened by a cacophony: long, loud hoots from cars, pick-ups and *tuk-tuks*, and clamorous crackles and explosions from fireworks. he rose and went to his room in the hotel. Jun had not returned.